DEVICES BRIGHTLY SHINING

MAGNIFICENT DEVICES · BOOK NINE

SHELLEY ADINA

Moonshell
Books

Cover design by Kalen O'Donnell. Images from Shutterstock.com, used under license, and the author's collection.

Author font by Anthony Piraino at OneButtonMouse.com

Devices Brightly Shining / Shelley Adina—2nd ed.

ISBN 978-1-939087-37-9

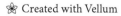 Created with Vellum

The Magnificent Devices series

Lady of Devices
Her Own Devices
Magnificent Devices
Brilliant Devices
A Lady of Resources
A Lady of Spirit
A Lady of Integrity
A Gentleman of Means
Devices Brightly Shining (Christmas novella)
Fields of Air
Fields of Iron
Fields of Gold

Carrick House (novella)
Selwyn Place (novella)
Holly Cottage (novella)
Gwynn Place (novella)

The Mysterious Devices series

The Bride Wore Constant White
The Dancer Wore Opera Rose
The Matchmaker Wore Mars Yellow
The Engineer Wore Venetian Red
The Judge Wore Lamp Black
The Professor Wore Prussian Blue

Merry Christmas to all
from Lady Claire and the flock

**Book 9 of the Magnificent Devices series—
a short Christmas sugarplum!**

On the first day of Christmas
My true love gave to me
Dreadful relations, high expectations,
And a sudden urge to pull up ropes and flee.

It is the event of the season—on Twelfth Night, the Dunsmuirs have invited the cream of London society to celebrate the marriage of Lady Claire Trevelyan and Andrew Malvern at a reception to which the Prince Consort himself is expected. Captain Ian Hollys brings his fiancée Alice Chalmers to attend and meet his family—people who cannot see past her flight boots to the woman who stands by his side as an equal.

When two young cousins of Gloria Meriwether-Astor arrive in London, the inhabitants of Carrick House are happy to welcome them. Sydney and Hugh Meriwether-Astor are completing a world tour, and the Dunsmuirs' ball is just the thing to cap it off in splendid fashion. But Maggie learns that Sydney has his own plans for the family business. And unlike Gloria, said plans don't include cutting off the supply of arms to the Royal Kingdom of Spain and the Californias.

It's time for Alice—someone with a spine, an airship of her own, and reasons to put fields of air between herself and decisions about her future—to pull up ropes and warn Gloria that betrayal is closer than she thinks …

"Some very nice challenges and examination of sexism of the era. There's the obvious—all of the women are planning their own lives. Even better, they're all planning different lives, different paths—because there's more than one way for a woman to live and be strong and express her agency... The books are already turning into far more than Claire's story and I'm happy to see that." —Fangs for the Fantasy, on *Devices Brightly Shining*

DEVICES BRIGHTLY SHINING

CHAPTER 1

The third day of Christmas
1894
Hollys Park, Somerset

The invitation did not come by pneumatic tube, the usual means of delivery employed by the Royal Mail, but by a personal courier dressed in the Dunsmuir livery, who was piloting a two-piston steam landau of a respectable vintage.

He presented the envelope to Alice Chalmers with a flourish, and then puttered away down the long drive of Hollys Park, frightening several quail and three of Ian's imported French hens out of the drive and under the hedge into the pear orchard.

Alice closed the front door and went into the morning room to open it.

The creamy paper was as heavy as satin, the words engraved at no small expense.

Earl and Countess Dunsmuir
request the honor of your presence
at a reception celebrating the recent marriage of
Dr. and Mrs. Andrew Malvern
Hatley House, London
on Twelfth Night at eight o'clock
Evening dress

Captain Ian Hollys called from the hall, "Alice? Are you in here?"

"In the morning room," she said, and a moment later he joined her.

"I saw a landau as I was crossing the park. Did the invitation come?"

She handed it to him by way of reply, and he scanned the curling, elegant lines. "It doesn't say whether His Royal Highness the Prince Consort is to attend."

"We know he is—he told Claire he wanted a wedding dance with her." The thought of being in the same room with Queen Victoria's husband was both awe-inspiring and terrifying. He was one of the foremost engineers of the age, and the patron of the Royal Society of Engineers, of which Andrew Malvern was an honored member. So was Claire a member, for that matter, having been inducted the summer just past.

In some ways Alice was as comfortable in their company as a foot is in a familiar shoe. But in other, more personal ways, she was not.

The stepdaughters of air pirates simply didn't converse with princes, though Claire had told her for true that His Highness wished a word with the future Lady Hollys and the co-inventor of the Zeppelin Automaton Intelligence System.

In other words, herself. Somehow that was the strangest thing of all.

Alice's mind veered away from the contemplation of it, and turned to more familiar, congenial things. "Are you coming out to *Swan* this morning?" she asked the man she had promised to marry.

Ian was wearing his estate clothes, consisting of a clean but uncollared shirt, tweed pants, and sturdy walking boots. On the lapel of his ancient tweed jacket he had pinned a sprig of holly with a few bright red berries, as a nod to the season. He looked the very picture of a contented country squire—minus the girth and plus the gray-eyed good looks that even now made her pulse speed up.

How was it possible that she was to be his wife? She, mechanic Alice Chalmers, formerly of the Texican Territory, daughter of a desert flower and a spy, to be Lady Hollys at some hazy future date that she had managed so far not to name?

"No," he said. "If we are to go to London for the reception, I must see my steward and give instructions to have the farming equipment seen to. With this hard frost, the boilers may crack, and that will mean no end of trouble in the spring."

"So we are going, then," she said, half hoping he would change his mind and say no. "Even though we've only just returned from their wedding."

"Of course we are going." He left off fussing with his jacket and gazed at her in some surprise. "Claire is your closest friend, is she not? Why would we not go?"

"No reason at all," Alice said.

Lady Claire Malvern, nee Trevelyan, was the closest thing

to a sister Alice had ever known. And she had married the one man on earth whom Alice felt could possibly be worthy of her. They were well matched in intelligence, spirit, and compassion, and Alice had long ago gotten over her brief *tendre* for that same gentleman in the realization that for him, there was no other woman alive but Claire.

Just as, for some inexplicable reason, there now seemed to be no other woman alive for Ian but herself. Which made her deliriously happy on most days, and utterly frightened on others.

"Then I shall send a note to my sister in Mayfair," he said briskly, "and tell her to expect us on the third of January."

Alice's fingers lost their ability to function and the invitation fluttered to the Aubusson carpet. "I thought we would stay at Carrick House. I always have. Other than *Swan*, it's the closest thing I have to a home."

He smiled and took her shoulders in both hands, pulling her close. "We have been tucked away in the country for long enough, my dear. With the demise of the Venetian assassin, there is no longer any danger to your life. It is time for you to meet my family and take your place in society as my intended. I suspect that in Lady Dunsmuir's mind, this reception for Claire and Andrew is to function rather as your coming-out in that regard. I must remember to hunt up Mother's jewelry for you."

"What if I don't want to come out?" Alice said a little desperately. "What if I want to stay right here until we're married?"

"Once that happens, you'll still need to be presented," he pointed out. "Meeting the prince at a less formal occasion will be good practice."

"You make it sound like a dance lesson."

"It is, rather. Buck up, darling. If Claire can do it, so can you."

"Claire was born to it," Alice said stubbornly. "I, as you know, wasn't."

"And for that I thank heaven," Ian told her with tenderness. "Any other woman would not have been able to save my life. You must cease looking at yourself as somehow less than the women of our acquaintance, Alice. Claire herself has told me often enough that if she had the choice of facing certain death with me or with you at her side, she would choose you without hesitation."

Alice couldn't help but smile at that. "I hope you aren't offended."

"How could I be, when I share her opinion? Come now. The prince is no monster, and my sister and her daughters no dragons. I do not much care for Joan's choice of husband, but since he outranks me I cannot complain about it—in his hearing, at least."

The seventh day of Christmas

On New Year's Day, Alice and Ian and her crew boarded *Swan*, whose return to life and use from the graveyard of lost ships following Alice's close call in Venice was nearly completed. Alice and Ian and anyone else they could rope into helping had focused their restoration efforts in two areas: the living quarters, which Alice presently occupied since of course she could not live unmarried in the manor house with Ian; and the engine room. Work in the latter had spread into the attached navigation gondola, and while the cosmetic side of the repairs was not yet complete, at least Alice could be confident that *Swan* would not fall out of the sky for want of functioning gears and steam.

After a smooth flight that went a long way toward settling her spirits, they moored at the Carrick Airfield in Vauxhall Gardens, much to the delight of her navigator, Jake Fletcher McTavish. The snow-covered field itself belonged to Lady Claire, having once been a large expanse pitted with blast craters next to the cottage in which she and her orphan charges had lived. Now the visitor saw a bustling commercial enterprise, with smooth, level landing berths; steam vehicles to take passengers back and forth to London proper; a ground crew to moor and tie down visiting airships; and a fleet office where mechanical pigeons could be rented to carry messages between ships on their voyages.

It was all managed by Jake's half-brother Stephen, known to one and all as Snouts, on account of his decidedly protuberant nose. Jake turned to Alice as they disembarked, clearly having seen Snouts's gangly figure in the distance.

"Permission to take land leave, Captain?" he asked. "I'll be glad to see everyone at Carrick House again."

They had not discussed the subject, but it was clear that Jake had no intention of joining their family party at Lord and Lady Blount's townhouse in Mayfair. Alice suspected that her navigator would feel about as happy to be there as the Blounts would be happy to have him should they discover his history as a cutpurse, cosher, and all-round dab hand in a scrape.

The thought of being without him after five years of sailing together (not counting his time in the Venetian underwater prison), even if it was only for a week, made her feel bereft, as though she were wearing an empty holster.

"Granted," she said. "Wish I could come with you."

Jake nodded, making sure that Ian, now supervising the loading of valises into a landau, was well out of earshot. "Chin up. Maybe they'll be civil, and not like proper toffs at all. The captain turned out all right, didn't he?"

With these bracing words, he jogged off to rescue his rucksack before it joined the valises, and a few minutes later the four of them were puttering over the bridge. London met them with a roar and a clatter, the streets crowded with steam drays and buses, bells clanging and engines and vehicles darting this way and that. But for all the cacophony of commerce, one could still see evidence of the season—a holly wreath upon a warehouse door, a fir garland gaily decking the side of a dray loaded with barrels of ale. Alice's party became part of the mechanical river that washed them all too soon into the quieter confines of Mayfair.

Christmastide bells rang the hour of four o'clock as the vehicle decanted them outside 17 Hanover Square, the valises were unloaded, and then Snouts and Jake racketed off, waving, in the direction of Belgravia and Claire and Andrew's home, Carrick House.

Alice took a deep breath and manufactured a smile for Ian's sake.

A stout individual in severe black livery met them at the door, which had been decked with the biggest wreath of fir cones and red and gold ribbon that Alice had ever seen. "Captain Hollys. Miss Chalmers. You are welcome indeed."

"Hello, Wilson. You may call my fiancée Captain Chalmers. How are you keeping?" Ian said easily as footmen appeared and vanished with their luggage.

"Er … yes, sir. Tolerably well, thank you, sir. You will find her ladyship and the young ladies in the parlor once you have refreshed yourselves. Please follow me."

They had been in the air barely an hour, and in the landau less than that, but Alice supposed it would be bad form to appear before one's hostess in flight jacket, canvas pants, a leather corselet, and a linen shirt that had never seen a pressing iron in its life. She realized rather belatedly that she was going to have to wear a skirt every single day she was here, and she only owned the one.

Maybe that was what Claire had meant by shopping for her trousseau. Another skirt would probably come in handy once *Swan* was fully restored and she was spending more time at Hollys Park doing … whatever ladies did.

The butler showed them to their rooms. Ian's was down at the end, overlooking what remained of the garden in this season of dormancy, and Alice's was on the other side of the corridor, close to the head of the stairs. "The young ladies are next to you, Miss—er, Captain Chalmers, and I am bidden to tell you that if you are in need of the fripperies and furbelows beloved of females, you may apply to them."

"Thank you." Any hopes of finding sensible company in her future nieces-in-law was fading fast. But then, they were a good four or five years younger than her twenty-four, so she supposed allowances had to be made.

After she had put on a white waist with a little tucking and embroidery down the front, and her chestnut-brown skirt, she attempted to twist up her hair the way Claire did. A couple of tortoiseshell pins rammed in on either side would ensure the curly mass didn't fall into her teacup, and she didn't bother to take off her boots. No one would see her feet under the skirt and petticoat, anyway.

She met Ian at the head of the staircase, where he'd clearly been waiting for her. "All right?" She did a little pirouette.

"You look a perfect picture, as Maggie would say." He gave her a kiss that made her blush, and then offered her his arm. "Shall we? I cannot wait to introduce you to my family."

A footman pushed open double doors painted in gray and gold, and they swept in.

"Ian!" A woman two or three years older than he rose from the sofa and crossed the room, her beringed hands outstretched in welcome. "I am so happy to see you."

She shared his dark hair, gray eyes, and firmness of chin, Alice saw at once. But there the resemblance ended. She was corseted to an uncomfortable degree in the fashion of the day, with a regal bosom enhanced by an acre of lace and embroidery and pearl necklaces heaped one upon another. She may have cut quite a figure among her peers, but the ability to hug someone was definitely impaired by the ensemble.

Ian embraced her as well as he could, and her oriental rose scent enveloped them both as he stepped aside and took Alice's hand. "Joan, may I introduce my fiancée, Captain Alice Chalmers. Alice, this is my sister, Joan, Lady Blount."

Alice received a hug and the distinct sensation that she would be wearing Lady Blount's scent until her next opportunity for a bath.

"And these are my daughters. Frances is the elder, in the green frock, and Lillian the younger by a year."

Two young ladies came forward, smiling and curious. "Welcome, Miss Chalmers." They kissed her in turn and then turned to Ian. "Uncle Ian, how lovely to see you. Congratulations upon your engagement."

Well, this was a cordial beginning. Maybe it wouldn't be so

bad after all. The girls were a little older than Maggie and Lizzie, carrying themselves with the elegance of good breeding and expensive schools. Lillian's hair was as red and curly as her sister's was smooth and dark, and both wore it up in the pompadour style, rippling in waves over forehead and temples and drawing the attention to long-lashed blue eyes, creamy skin, and … what was the term? Oh yes—bee-stung lips.

"Shall we have tea?" Lady Blount inquired, and they seated themselves upon sofa and settee while she poured the tea into thin china cups without a drop going astray. Shortbread and thin slices of fruitcake, luscious with cherries and nuts, were handed round.

"Where is Donald, Joan?" Ian inquired. "I had thought he would be here to greet us. I haven't seen him in a year at least."

"I expected him back from his club an hour ago myself. But that is Donald—let him within a mile of his cronies in his club and it becomes difficult to extricate him."

One could see one's cronies any day of the week, but being on hand to greet one's visiting family? Alice couldn't imagine a situation other than prison that would keep her from seeing her father and his wife and her little half-sisters if they were to come within five hundred miles.

While Lady Blount inquired after her brother's health, Alice became aware of the gazes of the young ladies, fixed upon her own feet with fascination. At last Frances's wondering gaze lifted to meet that of Alice. "I declare, Miss Chalmers, I never thought to see such a thing in Mama's parlor. How brave you are."

"See what?" Alice inspected the floor. "Have I brought in mud? Or a beetle?"

"You're wearing boots!" Frances whispered, as though it were a scandal.

Maybe it was.

Alice tucked her feet as far under her as she could, smoothing down her skirt. "They're comfortable, and the only other shoes I have are the flimsy ones that go with my dinner dress."

"You have only two pairs of shoes?" Lillian's china-plate eyes widened. "Oh, my dear."

"Girls," Lady Blount said, "one's habiliments are not a suitable topic for mixed company."

"But Mama, you would never allow us to wear boots and buckles to tea," Lillian objected.

"Allowances must be made for guests," her ladyship said firmly. "Miss Chalmers's feet are not your concern. Have another slice of cake."

"Captain Chalmers," Alice said automatically.

"I beg your pardon?" The lady did not use a lorgnette, but the effect upon nose and eyebrows was the same.

"Alice prefers to be addressed as Captain rather than Miss," Ian said. "And frankly, since I am addressed as Captain Hollys rather than Sir Ian, I find it difficult to justify why she should not be as well."

"A woman addressed as Captain?" Lady Blount seemed to be having difficulty taking in the concept. "I have never heard of such a thing."

"Neither has the Admiralty, apparently," Alice said, offering a smile. "When I went to register my ship, I was informed that while I could do so and allow a gentleman to captain her, I could not become a serving member of the Royal Aeronautic Corps and captain her myself."

"Which did not go over well, as you may imagine," Ian said with a frown.

"Join the Corps," Frances repeated, when it became clear her mother could not.

"But they're all *men*," Lillian added.

"They are now," Alice agreed, "but I suspect the day may come when they find they are losing talented, capable aeronauts by excluding half the population."

"But why would any female *want* to be included?" Lillian persisted. "I can't imagine anything more appalling."

"Not everyone has your imagination," Alice said, doing her best to be polite.

"I beg your pardon." Affronted, Lillian picked up her teacup and turned her shoulder toward Alice.

She resisted the urge to apologize. *She* had not just insulted both of her guests and not even been aware of it. Were all society people like this? Did Claire have to deal with this sort of thing?

And then Alice remembered that Claire did indeed have to. Alice had seen it herself during the preparations for her wedding at Gwynn Place at Christmas. Alice imagined that Lady Flora St. Ives Jermyn loved her daughter, but from the incessant commentary upon her person, her choices, and the underlying implication that Claire was marrying beneath her —had someone spilled the beans that Claire had turned down Ian's proposal all those months ago?—Alice could see why her friend spent as little time as possible in her mother's company.

Alice had so hoped that she would be accepted by Ian's family despite her foibles and her lack of connections. Who could have imagined that within two minutes, a pair of laced and buckled flight boots would put the kibosh on that?

CHAPTER 2

LONDON

The seventh day of Christmas

Dearest sister Lizzie and cousin Maggie,

As you know, I'm not much for gossip, but now and again I come into so much news that I simply must share, or burst.

Do you recall our cousin Evan Douglas, who had been conducting experiments with dream images for my late unlamented father? He still has not got over the part he played in that affair at Colliford Castle, and I suspect this is the lion's share of the reason he declined the invitation to Lady Claire's wedding. The other part is that the poor chap hasn't a life outside the laboratory.

However, since he is in Town for the presentation of some dull paper or other, I have made it my mission to rectify the situation, and beg you to secure an invitation for him to the grand razzle at Hatley House on Twelfth Night. Isn't it a splendid idea? I imagine he will not think so, but I implore you to ensure the poor stick has a good time. For my part, I will see that he turns up appropriately dressed, and smelling of cologne and not noxious chemicals.

Since I inherited my father's membership at the Gaius Club, we

14

shall take rooms there. I do hope we can see the two of you—are you at home this week? Do tell by return tube.

In other news, while I was in Paris this past autumn you will never guess whom I met. Go on. Take a moment.

No guesses?

Then I shall tell you—none other than Gloria Meriwether-Astor's cousin, Sydney Meriwether-Astor. He and his younger brother Hugh have been on a trip around the globe via steamship, if you can imagine it. Such fogies! But full of dash and go nonetheless —they have had many an adventure, and have now washed up on the shores of Old Blighty, staying at Brown's Hotel.

Fuddy-duddies—they clearly do not know that gentlemen of fashion buy temporary memberships to the Gaius Club and stay there. But this is information to which young ladies are not to be privy, so I shall button my lips!

They are madly interested in becoming acquainted with the friends of their cousin. Their late father, I believe, was that criminal Gerald's younger brother, but being the son of a criminal myself, I cannot find it in my heart to blame them for their relations.

Do please ask Lady Dunsmuir if her guest list may accommodate them also?

You know as well as I that the party will be an utter crush, but that is to be expected with the social event of the year. They simply must be there, if only to take a report back to Philadelphia for their cousin to enjoy.

Do let me know. I am perishing for the sight of both of you!

Your brother (and cousin)

Claude Seacombe

*L*ady Claire Malvern folded up Claude's letter with a merry laugh, and handed it back to Lizzie. "I am no prophet, but it is difficult to believe that boy will ever settle down and become the sensible shipping-company president his grandpapa wished him to be. Such language!"

Lizzie smiled and fanned herself with the letter, full of Claude's characteristic italics and dashes, as the three of them took tea next to the fire. Claire was grateful for a rare moment of peace before the room filled with children looking for their slice of cake or plate of sandwiches, which Mrs. Morven and Granny Protheroe never failed to supply, knowing the ravenous appetites of growing bodies.

"Have you heard from your grandmother recently?" Claire asked.

Lizzie and Maggie shook their heads. "I have a feeling she is not recovering very quickly from our grandfather's passing," Maggie said. "But as you know, she is not forthcoming with her own emotions, so any letters we do receive are little more than weather reports, complaints about the maids, or accounts of who has called lately."

"All of which have been equally dull. At least she's addressing them to the two of us now," Lizzie pointed out. "That's progress."

Maggie rolled her eyes. "Such are the benefits of discovering my parents' marriage lines and of my being declared legitimate," she said wryly. "I am now being named in her correspondence, just like a real person."

Claire stroked Maggie's glossy hair, which today was drawn into a neat chignon that still, in all its simplicity, managed to look extremely fashionable. "Do not allow bitterness into your heart, dearest," she said softly. "It will only act like the worm inside an apple, and do no harm to *her* whatsoever."

Maggie shook her head, and Claire's hand fell away. "I don't," she said. "She is what she is, and if her health fails, at least I will have nothing to reproach myself with. She had no relationship with my mother, either, from all accounts, but at least my parents had each other."

"And you have Polgarth, and your work with genetics, and your aunts and cousins," Lizzie said. "I'd much rather have been a product of your side of the family … but then I would not have Claude and Evan, would I?"

"Or the prospect of running the Seacombe Shipping Company yourself," Maggie pointed out. "Because you know quite well that Claude is not settling to it, and Grandmother is at her wits' end. He will wind up being the figurehead in the corner office, and you will be the one actually doing the work."

"Not likely," Lizzie said with a snort. "We three will share that office, see if we don't. I want my own desk, with a brass plaque bearing my name."

"You may have mine. I shall be setting up a laboratory of my own once I graduate from university. Or perhaps even before that, if I can persuade Grandfather to come in with me."

"I will rent you a warehouse for it, then, at a very attractive price."

Maggie stuck out her tongue at her cousin and threw a grape at her head.

"Girls, good heavens," Claire objected. "I am very glad the younger children are not here to see this display."

Unrepentant, Lizzie picked the grape from her hair and popped it into her mouth.

"You must write to Davina this evening and tell her of these new guests." Claire returned to the subject, refreshing their teacups. "While there will indeed be a crush, three young gentlemen of means and prospects will likely be very welcome. Still, she ought to know they are coming, in order that we may all acknowledge the connection. Our friendship with Gloria is very valuable to me. Oh, how I wish she could have come to this, at least, even if she could not attend the wedding."

The door opened and Snouts, Jake, and Lewis loped in, followed by the younger children—all former street sparrows, and all being educated and fitted for a useful place in society by Claire and Andrew. In the general merriment and greetings and catching-up and making of plans, Claire was distracted, but before bed she did manage to send a note over to Hatley House, since Lizzie and Maggie had not. And when she closed the little door to the pneumatic system and turned, Andrew took her into his arms, and then there was neither time nor desire for anything but him.

The eighth day of Christmas

In the morning, she and Andrew appeared for breakfast when everyone else was nearly finished. Self-consciously, Claire tucked an errant tendril of hair into her hasty chignon and hoped that she was not blushing too fervently. Honestly, must everyone look at their plates as though they had never seen a newlywed before?

"Has there been a note from Hatley House?" she inquired

of the room in general, buttering a slice of toast for Andrew while he busied himself slathering raspberry jam on one for her.

"Not yet, but something came from Alice," Lewis told her, handing over a folded bit of crested stationery. "She and Captain Hollys are staying in Mayfair."

Claire paused in the opening of the note. "Lewis, you will see that the house covers any charges that Claude and Evan incur at the Gaius Club?"

Lewis, unbeknownst to any but the inhabitants of Carrick House, owned the fashionable club frequented by the younger set in London. "Of course, Lady," he said. "I've already taken care of it. Excluding any gambling, I assume?"

"Yes." She gave him a look over a pair of imaginary spectacles. "And if there is any way to minimize poor Claude's losses, I trust you will find it."

"A timely interruption usually works," Snouts drawled. "A message, a young lady asking for the wrong person, that sort of thing."

"I leave the means to you." Claire smiled at them with affection and directed her attention to Alice's note.

Dearest Claire,

I hope you are settled into Carrick House again and that people have got used to calling you Mrs. Malvern. Ian and I are with his sister, Lady Blount, and her husband and daughters at 17 Hanover Square, and looking forward to Twelfth Night.

I would love to call at your earliest convenience. Do you have an hour to help me find a proper pair of shoes? And another skirt? I know you're busy, but this is an emergency.

19

Love to Andrew. Don't tell him I am all in a welter. I am ashamed of myself, and if he knew, Ian would be too.

Alice

Hanover Square? Number 17? Good heavens—if memory served, Ian's sister was living in Lord James Selwyn's old home! Claire's late fiancé had lived considerably above his means in taking the house; she hoped Lord Blount was not similarly burdened. Goodness. She would have to tell Mrs. Morven, who had cooked for him there, of the new connection.

Claire had a list of a hundred things that must be seen to—arranging for the purchase of the warehouse next to Andrew's laboratory in Orpington Close chief among them, to say nothing of seeing Maggie and Lizzie back to Munich for their final term of sixth form suitably outfitted and supplied. But Alice and fashion were paired as uncomfortably as ever Claire had been during the days of Mama's thwarted attempts at launching her into society. One could do nothing but empathize ... and offer all the assistance one could.

So a tube was dispatched, and that afternoon Alice presented herself in Claire's study, the very picture of despair.

"Claire, I can't tell you how much this means to me." She subsided on the sofa, pulling her feet up under her and then thinking better of it and setting them decorously upon the floor. "The looks on those girls' faces at breakfast when I suggested a shopping trip—I felt as though I were three years old and they didn't relish the prospect of cleaning the jam off my chin."

Claire set her teeth at the thought of anyone slighting Alice, whose intelligence was formidable, and whose bravery had saved Claire's life at no small risk to her own. "I should think that young ladies would enjoy a trip to New Bond Street. Shopping is an acquired taste for some, however."

"But you always look so neat, and appropriate, and wear pretty hats." Alice's eyes held curiosity. "Don't tell me you had to acquire the taste?"

Claire nodded, remembering her trials at the hands of London's then leading modiste. "I found my mother's taste very difficult to bear. Even now, my own extends only to embroidery and cutwork, and shudders away from ruffles, flounces, and ruching of any kind. And we will not even discuss the color pink."

"I don't mind embroidery. But what on earth is cutwork?"

For answer, Claire extended her arm and indicated the sleeve of her buff-colored walking dress.

"Ah. Well, that's pretty enough. I'd probably tear it on a pipe as soon as look at it, though."

"One doesn't wear cutwork in the engine room, dearest. Now come. We have an arduous task ahead of us. I am pleased that at least you are wearing a corset. That, I am reliably informed, is the foundation of style."

Claire waited until they were closeted in the dressing-rooms of her favorite shop in Beauchamp Place, hoping that the act of disrobing would produce in her friend an equal degree of honesty. "That skirt is perfect on you, Alice," she said when the latter emerged. "You are tall enough to carry off the fantail and the soutache at once."

"Is that what this ribbon trim is called?"

"Yes. You must have a waist to go with it. Try this one." She handed her a very pretty embroidered waist and Alice retreated behind the screen. "I am curious as to why you feel you must accommodate these nieces of Ian's, though. Surely the woman who is received by the Empress of Prussia does not care two pins for the opinions of girls barely out of school?"

Silence, but for the rustling of batiste and fine wool. Then, "I want his family to like me."

"Of course they like you. How could they not?"

Alice came out, looking first to Claire for approval, and then into the mirror. "Well." She turned this way and that. "I suppose this is all right, isn't it?"

"It looks lovely. I advise immediate purchase, with the skirt in both the blue with cream trim, and the hunter green with navy. But you have not answered me."

Once more behind the screen, Alice accepted without demur the afternoon dress Claire passed her. "If I'm going to marry Ian, I have to get along with his family. And that means making friends with his sister and nieces."

"It seems to me your initial efforts would be directed toward Lady Blount. One's circle does not usually include the very young."

"Yours does."

"Maggie and Lizzie are different."

"I'll say." An unladylike snort came from behind the delicately painted panels. "I'll bet it would never occur to Frances or Lillian to shoot the hull out of an undersea dirigible and sink it. Or to find a way to divert a missile so that it didn't scuttle a royal airship."

"I think that highly likely," Claire said. "But I feel rather sorry for them if that is the case. What is your relationship with Lady Blount thus far?"

"She is pleasant enough at the table, but other than that, I haven't seen much of her. She is busy with Yuletide calls, and is a few years older than Ian, you know."

"So there you are in the middle, between a lady of a certain age and her daughters of a certain sensibility. But dearest, think of the connection in practical terms. How often are you going to see them, really?"

"That's not the point." Alice came out wearing the afternoon dress, a silvery gray with cutwork underlain in satin a foot deep along the hem, and matching cutwork over the bosom. "Good grief, Claire, when am I ever going to wear this?"

"When people call at Hollys Park and you offer them tea," Claire suggested. "Or when you visit the families in the neighborhood for your wedding calls. That is customary, you know. My mother spent two months visiting everyone she knew all around St. Just in Roseland, despite the fact it was her second marriage."

Alice looked appalled. "Do I have to?"

She might as well know the truth. "No, you do not have to. But where is one to make a beginning if one is to build relationships with people you will be seeing for the rest of your life?"

"Like your mother, Ian already has relationships with everyone in the county, I'm sure."

"But his relationships will be different from yours. Who will organize church fetes and harvest dinners and aid to the poor?"

"The minister's wife?" Alice asked faintly.

"You will be Lady Hollys, the first lady in the neighborhood," Claire reminded her with pointed gentleness. "Has no one told you what the job entailed?"

"I don't think Ian knows about the harvest dinners."

"He very likely does not. His mother would have quietly organized everything and he would simply have enjoyed the results."

"Have you ever done any of those things?"

"No, but I am not going to be Lady Hollys. I am Mrs. Malvern, whose life—thank heavens—is quite different. My mother, however, has done those and more, which is why I know about them."

"And why you turned down the job?" Alice attempted to retreat once more behind the screen, as if she was ashamed the words had escaped her, but Claire did not allow her to hide.

"Try this coat in the darker gray."

"I don't need a coat."

"It is January, Alice. You will need a coat in which to pay calls. And no, church fetes and harvest dinners had nothing to do with my decision where Ian was concerned. We were not suited, and there was an end to it."

"I'm beginning to wonder if we're not, either," Alice mumbled as she shoved her arms into the coat and allowed Claire to do up the buttons.

"Very nice." Claire asked the hovering clerk for the hat to match, and when it came, stood back to admire her handiwork. "You must have both."

"The hat too?"

"The hat too, and another dress."

"Claire, I can't. This is going to cost a fortune."

"You have a fortune. Or will. We will put it all on Ian's account. That is, unless you plan to do a runner and pull up ropes before it is all delivered?"

Alice was silent for so long as she removed the gray and put on a claret-colored tea gown that Claire had a moment to fear that she actually meant to break her engagement.

"The lace over the bosom is very pretty, Alice. And that color brings out the bloom in your cheeks, like a milkmaid in a meadow."

"A milkmaid wouldn't be wearing this. I still need shoes."

"I know just the place."

"I'm not going to do a runner." Alice gazed at herself in the glass, touching the lace as though she had never worn any before and wasn't sure how it should lie. "But I'm coming to the conclusion that neither he nor I have thought this through."

"Do you love him?"

Her gaze met that of Claire in the mirror. "More than anything. But it seems that's only the beginning. It took you and Andrew five years to reconcile yourselves to marriage."

Claire tried not to wince. "That sounds as though we were unwilling, or forced. But in another sense 'reconcile' is the right word. We needed to be fitted together. To have the jagged bits smoothed off and the hollow parts filled in. I suppose our adventures contributed to that, but even in Munich, as recently as October, the process was still not complete—inside both of us, where it counts most."

"Perhaps Ian and I are at the beginning of that process. I'm all jagged bits, I'm afraid, and he still has a few hollow parts. I certainly don't fit into the hole his mother left, and I'm beginning to despair that I ever will."

Claire crossed the room and put a hand on her sleeve. "No one expects you to fit into her place, my friend. One creates one's own. Ian, I am sure, is no more like his father than he is like his sister. His place is his own, and yours is, too. You simply have to discover how to fill your places together, as Andrew and I have. As we still are."

Alice eyed her. "Is marriage hard, then? Is that what you're saying?"

Claire could not stop the smile that spread over her face. "Oh, no. It is as easy as laughter, as effortless as steering before a good wind. But at the same time—speaking from my vast experience of nine days—it is a territory that has never been navigated before by the two of us."

"Aren't you afraid?"

Claire's smile widened as joy welled up in her heart and spilled over. "Not in the least. No matter what may come, past events have made sure that we know the measure of one another. And there is enormous safety in knowing that in fair weather and foul, we are sailing together."

Alice's lower lip trembled, and her eyes filled. Claire couldn't help it—she took her friend into her arms and gave her a hug. "What is it, dearest?"

"I'm just so happy that you're happy," Alice whispered. "It's all I ever wanted for you. I only hope that—" Her throat seemed to close.

"You will have the same happiness," Claire promised softly. "It is a course worth setting, bumps and all. And you are not alone. You have us. As Maggie used to say, we're a flock."

At which point, to Claire's utter dismay, Alice began to cry in earnest.

CHAPTER 3

When the hatboxes and dress boxes were delivered later that afternoon, there was no end of consternation in Hanover Square when they were all discovered to be marked with Alice's name.

"This must be a mistake," Frances said blankly. "For one, we cannot yet patronize Beauchamp Place until Papa increases our allowance, and two, there are ever so many."

Alice was rather amazed at the number of boxes herself—did each glove and individual shoe have its own container? She may not have decided the important question of whether or not she and Ian were suited, but she had decided one thing —she was not going to let this houseful of females ride roughshod over her any more. Over a refreshing cup of tea at the Savoy with Claire, a little of what her friend called spine seemed to have been transmitted along with petits fours and cream, the presence of her friend reminding her of her own best self.

"It isn't a mistake," Alice informed Frances airily, lifting a lid to peek at a lovely pair of gray suede shoes with what she had been told were kitten heels. They did not look in the least like kittens, but they were equally adorable. "You aren't the only female in the house who enjoys a little fashion. Wilson," she said to the hovering butler, "will you see these up to my room?"

"Certainly, Captain." He bustled off to summon the footman, leaving Alice feeling rather pleased that her ability to command had also returned to her.

By now Lillian had joined them, and was actually tugging at the ribbons of a hatbox. "Is this mine? I wasn't expecting it for days yet."

"No," Frances said with some asperity. "This entire heap is from Beauchamp Place and is for Alice. Captain Chalmers," she corrected herself sweetly.

"You may call me Alice," she said, as though making a great concession. "We are to be family. You don't call your uncle Captain, I'm sure."

"Neither do I call you aunt."

Alice drew a breath. Snooty little snippet. "I would think not, since I am not yet married to your uncle. When I am, then you may."

"*If* you are."

Alice raised a brow. "Don't get your hopes up."

Her guns spiked, Frances took a moment to regroup, and Alice pressed the advantage.

"I don't know what you've got against me, since you never saw me in your life before yesterday. It can't be my boots, because that would make you shallow and petty, and I am certain that is not the case." She smiled with equal sweetness. "And it can't be that I am to marry your uncle, because we'll be living miles away with no nevermind to you. That would make you spiteful and irrational, which I am equally certain is not the case."

Frances and Lillian gaped at her, wide-eyed and speechless.

"So here is my proposal. You two keep a civil tongue in your heads, and I'll do my best to remember not to shoot you like the varmints you are. After Twelfth Night your uncle and I will return to Hollys Park. You can go about your business and we'll all forget we had to have this conversation, all right?"

Frances's gaze fell to Alice's hip, and with the smoothness of long familiarity, Alice pulled the lightning pistol she had made out of its specially sewn pocket in her chestnut skirt, where, despite the death of the Venetian assassin, it still resided.

Lillian gasped. "You would not really shoot us, you unfeminine brute!"

"Name-calling is much more unfeminine than bearing arms, and requires much less sense," Alice told her pleasantly. "I had expected you to be better brought up."

"How dare you!"

"Quite easily. I'm glad we had this little chat. I look forward to more civil exchanges in future."

Wilson appeared from behind a swinging baize-covered door with the footman in tow, and Alice gathered up her shoes, a couple of flat boxes of gloves, and a hatbox. She bore them away to her room with the conviction that, while she had had the last word, it wouldn't be long before those two either capitulated or came back for another volley.

In any case, Alice felt much better than she had when she'd come down to breakfast.

After the family had gone to bed, she and Ian, unchaperoned, enjoyed a few moments together on the sofa before the parlor fire. Gazing at the mantel, which was so burdened with garlands and sparkling ribbon and an entire Christmas village in miniature that it was surprising it did not bow in the middle, she decided to be honest with him.

"Ian, I have to tell you that I ran up a bill the size of a mountain today when I went shopping with Claire."

He drew back a little, eyebrows raised. "I do not know which surprises me more—the bill, or the fact that you went shopping at all. I did not know you were capable of such a thing."

"I didn't either. I've always hated frippery and corsets and all the nonsense ladies are obliged to put up with. But Claire is very sensible about it."

"How is one sensible about these things?"

"She treats clothes like—like putting on a uniform. Or armor. I'm not sure which. Each garment has a purpose beyond simply covering you up. One dress might serve to incite a certain attitude in the hearts of other women at tea. Another makes guests feel comfortable because it's pretty but not elaborate. And other things are just practical—I bought a coat because it's January and my flight jacket doesn't go with my new silvery afternoon dress."

"Good heavens. An afternoon dress? And silvery? What is the world coming to?"

Alice cuddled into him, her head on his broad shoulder. "Do you mind?"

"As long as you are content and pleased with your armor, I do not mind in the least." He gave a low chuckle. "The two of you never cease to intrigue me with the many facets of your friendship."

After a moment, she said, "There is something else. You may think me petty, but I don't want there to be anything unsaid between us."

"Petty? That is the last word I would use in connection with you."

"You may not think so in a moment." She told him about Frances and Lillian, from the boots to the kitten-heeled shoes. "I am sorry to wear you out with drawing-room dustups, but I wanted you to know."

"I am sorry you were subject to such rudeness," he said with no little heat. "I will speak to my sister."

"Please don't." She linked her fingers with his. "I doubt anything she could say would make a difference. They either accept me as a member of the family or they don't, but either way, it's mine to handle."

He was silent a moment, squeezing her hand. "Drawing-room dustups?"

"I pulled my pistol on them."

"Great Caesar's ghost. It came to that?"

"Sad to say."

"I wish I had been there."

"It wouldn't have happened if you had."

He embraced her, smiling against her lips, and for a blissful quarter of an hour, Alice forgot that there was any such thing as nieces, petty or otherwise.

The ninth day of Christmas

Not for the first time, Claire was grateful that, despite her fashion advice to Alice, she herself did not have to shop for a gown suitable for the Twelfth Night reception. A gown in which she would dance with the prince and provoke seething jealousy in people like Lady Julia Mount-Batting and Mrs. David Haliburton would require more skill than nearly all the London modistes possessed—and certainly more in the way of ready cash than Claire was willing to give up in aid of such a pursuit.

For Gloria had sent her a Worth gown from Paris for her wedding dress, and in accordance with tradition, she would wear it to her first social engagement as a married woman, at Hatley House three days hence.

These happy circumstances meant that she and Andrew had time to meet with the land agent and her solicitor to secure the second warehouse on Orpington Close. They had discussed the possibility of removing his laboratory to occupy a section of the Morton Glass Works, of which she was part owner, so as to be closer to the Carrick Airfield. But in the end, as Andrew said, land values in that neighborhood had risen, and they were more likely to gain the space they needed where he was already established, shabby and smelling of fish though it might be.

As Claire removed her hat in the vestibule at Carrick House, the sounds of merriment and the clink of spoons and dishes told her that they must have company in the parlor. Granny Protheroe, in whom the aging process seemed to have been reversed since taking up residence in Wilton Crescent, came through the door bearing an empty tray.

"Ah, you're home, milady. I trust all is in order?"

"Yes, Granny. We were able to sign the papers today, and Mr. Malvern may begin production on the Helios Membrane for *Athena* as soon as it pleases him." She smiled over her shoulder at Andrew, who brushed snowflakes from her coat and helped her out of it. "I feel as though there ought to be a pipe and drum corps to commemorate the occasion. Speaking of occasions, who are our visitors?"

"Lizzie's brother, and Mr. Evan Douglas, and his friends from the Fifteen Colonies. They arrived in London this morning, and have come to pay their respects."

"How delightful!" She took Andrew's hand. "Come, let us meet them."

Claude Seacombe spotted them as they walked through the door. "Lady Claire!" he exclaimed, bounding over to give her a bearlike hug. "I am so happy to see you. And Mr. Malvern, sir." He shook hands rather as though Andrew's arm were a pump handle, and Claire smothered a smile.

"It has only been ten days since we were last together, Claude dear," she said, looking expectantly toward his companions. "How the days fly when one is happily occupied." She turned to Lizzie and Maggie's cousin, with whom they had become acquainted the previous summer. "Mr. Douglas, you are most welcome."

The young scientist was, if anything, thinner and more awkward than she remembered him. "Am I, ma'am? Truly? For I cannot forget that—" He choked, unable to go on.

"And I cannot forget that you are Lizzie's and Maggie's family," she said gently, and hugged him. His tall body, so stiff and uncertain, relaxed a little, and he actually returned her hug. "We have determined that only happy memories shall lie in our mutual past, and I advise you to do the same whilst you are here."

He straightened, and she released him. At last the flicker of a smile appeared on a face that might be handsome if his hair had been properly cut, and if he paid the least bit of attention to the state of his clothes. But, she supposed, when one lived in the laboratory as much as he did, these considerations might be too much to expect. She of all people understood that.

"Come and let Lizzie get you some tea. You look famished." Smiling, she turned to see Andrew shaking the hands of their two remaining guests. "Are these the world travelers?"

"Yes indeed," Claude said. "Mr. and Mrs. Andrew Malvern, may I present Mr. Sydney Meriwether-Astor and his younger brother Hugh, the cousins of our dear friend Miss Gloria Meriwether-Astor."

Claire thought this was doing it up a little brown, since Claude had ignored Gloria in favor of his own group of friends during much of their time together in Venice, but she overlooked this trifle in the general bonhomie. Besides, the less Claude knew of what had really gone on there, the better for everyone, since the dear boy had never met a thought he had not immediately broadcast to all around him.

She extended her hand cordially to Sydney. "Welcome to London, sir, and to Carrick House."

He bowed over it courteously, as did his brother, murmuring compliments and thanks for their hospitality. She examined both young men with interest, searching their tanned faces for a resemblance to Gloria. But aside from their height and elegance—which was evident despite having traveled around the world by steamship, an accomplishment that had to have its onerous moments—she could find none.

Though in their own way, they were as good-looking as

34

Gloria, with high cheekbones, merry eyes, and mouths given to smiling. Sydney appeared to be about twenty-six, and Hugh a year or two younger. The latter sported a tumble of brown curls upon his forehead, and freckles that made him look younger still. The former seemed more conscious of the impression he was making, with his hair combed neatly and his cuffs immaculate. Gold cufflinks bore only a monogram, not the diamonds and such that had become popular among the wealthy set who frequented the Gaius Club.

She seated herself upon the sofa next to Lizzie and secured two pieces of Christmas fruitcake for herself and Andrew while Maggie poured their tea.

Or attempted to. For her ward's attention was clearly fixed upon Sydney's handsome face rather than the spout, and Claire had to move suddenly to stop her before the tea ran over into the saucer.

"Oh, Lady, I'm so sorry." Maggie blushed scarlet and put down the flowered china pot. "You will have no room for milk."

"I can think of things worse than black tea." A few sips left enough room for the milk and allowed Maggie to regain her composure. "Mr. Meriwether-Astor, I do hope you have not emptied the conversational coffers of tales of your adventures, for I confess I am most anxious to hear at least one."

"Do call me Sydney, Mrs. Malvern," he urged. "I feel as though we are acquainted already, from all my cousin has said of you."

"Sydney, then. And Hugh." She smiled at them both, but if Hugh was aware of it, she would be surprised. He was gazing at Maggie as though he had never seen a young lady before. Perhaps he hadn't—not in the last several months, at any rate.

"We left Philadelphia a year ago last autumn," Sydney said, "on the family steamship, heading south for the West Indies. From there we visited the southern reaches of the Royal Kingdom of Spain and the Californias in the southern Americas. We came round the Horn at the end of January. When we reached the Californias in the spring, we were welcomed by associates of my uncle—the Californios, don't you know."

"Is that a family name?" Lizzie asked. "It seems odd."

"No, it's a rank, a word that tells one what kind of person a man is—the way *Texican* tells one where a man is from and the kind of person he is."

"Or she is," Claire said, sipping her tea. "In either case, perhaps they are rather like the Bloods here."

"A close friend of ours is from the Texican Territory," Maggie offered. "You will meet her at the reception. She is an airship captain, engaged to Captain Ian Hollys, who commanded the Dunsmuirs' flagship, *Lady Lucy,* before his retirement."

"We look forward to the introduction," Sydney said with a smile, then went on with his tale. "Well, the Californios are filthy rich—they rather run society on that side of the continent, so I suppose they are like your Bloods. Each landowner commands tens of thousands of acres of land. Since the discovery of gold in that country, you can imagine the wealth at their disposal."

"I don't see what good it does them," Jake said from his place near the fire, leaning on the mantel as he slurped his tea. "Them Californios don't believe in progress—they think airships are a blasphemy against God and won't allow 'em to fly over. Me and Alice were practically run out of the country when we tried to land a cargo in Reno."

"As were we, some years ago," Lizzie said. "Never mind. We don't need their gold, do we?"

"You've been to the Californias?" Sydney said in surprise. "Fancy that, and you so young."

"I am seventeen in two months, thank you, and we've been all over," Lizzie told him with breezy nonchalance. "The Texican Territory, the Canadas, France, Venice—"

"Lizzie," Claire murmured. The less said of Venice, the better.

"Well, we have. Do go on, Sydney. Where did you go next?"

"To the Eastern kingdoms—the Land of the Rising Sun, China, Hind, then overland on the train through Arabia to Egypt, where a ship took us through the Straits of Gibraltar and thence to France and England. And here we are."

"That's quite a voyage," Andrew said with some admiration. "I understand the knowledge of mechanics in China and Hind rivals and may even surpass our own. Did you happen to see devices of extraordinary originality or usefulness?"

Sydney's fine forehead furrowed a little. "Can't say I did … but I'm afraid that what catches my attention is often the colorful or trivial." He laughed with self-deprecating good humor.

"There were those enormous mechanical elephants in Hind, Syd," his brother reminded him. "Rather like our—"

"Oops, watch your saucer," Sydney said, diving for the bit of china.

Claire had not seen any imminent spills, but clearly Sydney was used to watching out for his brother. "Mechanical elephants," she marveled. "What were they used for?" She squashed a momentary urge to lift in *Athena* and go to see such an extraordinary thing herself.

"Moving large objects, I believe, and for building," Hugh replied, settling back in his seat. "Though they use real elephants for the same purpose, so I am not certain why they felt the need to reproduce Nature."

"You sound like a Californio," his brother told him, smiling.

"I imagine that torque and pressure could be increased by the use of steam," Maggie offered quietly, "thus increasing the mechanical strength. And an automaton, you know, would not need to be rested, fed, or cared for. It could work indefinitely as long as it was properly maintained."

"You are quite right," Sydney said, and Maggie blushed again, this time with pleasure.

Oh dear. Claire was not so sure she wanted her girl to set such store by the opinions of a young man who would be on his way across the ocean in a few days' time. There were plenty of intelligent young men in England to see her good qualities. She did not need to look abroad—especially to those who admired the Bloods, wherever they were to be found.

With a pneumatic hiss and a metallic *thunk*, a tube landed in the study. "I'll get it!" young Charlie exclaimed, and dashed away, to return in a moment with an envelope bearing the Dunsmuir crest.

Dearest Claire,

I should be delighted to welcome any connection of Gloria's to our party, and of course dear Claude and Mr. Douglas too. You know our guests of honor are free to invite whomever they please. You did not have to apply to me, you goose.

To think our fete is the day after tomorrow! Will is beside himself with excitement at the thought that not only will his beloved

Lady and Mr. Malvern have their party, but His Royal Highness will attend. I have had confirmation from Buckingham Palace and am feeling rather excited myself.

I long to see you. We missed you and Andrew dreadfully at Balmoral—but I suppose one's honeymoon must take precedence!

Ever your
Davina

Claire looked up from the note, smiling. "That's settled, then. Lady Dunsmuir is delighted to welcome the four of you. I do hope that among your trunks and valises you have packed evening dress. She expects a very important guest."

"Of course, ma'am," Claude said. "One doesn't go gallivanting around the world—or even to Paris—without one's glad rags, does one?"

"Yes, one does," Evan mumbled, on his second cup of tea and his third sandwich.

"We were frequently in company in the Californias and in Hind," Sydney said as though he hadn't spoken. "In fact, we were invited to the opera in San Francisco to see Madame Tetrazzini herself."

"At least they don't object to music there," Lizzie said, and drained her teacup. "But the likelihood of any of us venturing to San Francisco, opera or not, is very low if we cannot go by modern means of transportation."

"Steam trains are very modern," Hugh pointed out.

"But they are poky slow compared to airships, and much less comfortable and quiet."

"She has you there, Hugh." Sydney's eyes crinkled with appreciation of the picture Lizzie made in her cornflower-blue skirt and lacy waist. "I look forward to enjoying more conversation with you, Miss Elizabeth—perhaps for the first waltz?"

Lizzie looked up at him in surprise, and Claire took the opportunity to say smoothly, "You will be looking forward to seeing Lieutenant Terwilliger at the ball, will you not, Lizzie? With the Dunsmuirs in town, he will have land leave."

"He does indeed, Lady Claire," she said primly, arranging her skirts. "We are to walk along the Embankment tomorrow evening, in fact, to see the tumblers leaping and doing their acrobatics. With your permission, of course."

"Let us make a party of it!" Claude exclaimed. "Unless you and Tigg would rather be spoony without witnesses, that is."

Lizzie forgot her dignity as a young lady and stuck out her tongue at him. "We do not spoon. And besides, Maggie and Jake are going with us. Of course you may come. Evan, you will too, will you not?"

"If you wish it, Lizzie, of course I will," Evan said.

"Perhaps Sydney and Hugh would enjoy it as well?" Lizzie looked at them expectantly.

"It sounds rather like fifth wheels would be unwelcome," Hugh said awkwardly, suddenly unable to look Maggie in the face.

Jake put down his cup and saucer. "What's that supposed to mean?"

Claire wondered if poor Maggie could blush any more deeply, and hastened to the rescue. "You mistake us, gentlemen. Lizzie, Maggie, Jake, Lewis, Tigg, and Stephen—they have all grown up together. Claude and Evan are family. There is no question of fifth wheels or pairs of wheels in the case, with the exception of Lizzie and Tigg, whose friendship is not only close, but honorable, and very much supported by those who love them."

She and Lizzie exchanged a smile at this very first hint of their understanding being made public outside the circle of the family. While it would be a year or more yet before Lizzie made her debut and they could officially declare themselves, and to go out in company as a courting couple, Claire saw no reason to forbid the exchange of letters or deny one the other's company. These were not children fresh from the schoolroom, with no experience of the world. The very opposite was true.

Their own hearts had been their guide through stormy seas indeed, and Claire could wish nothing more than to see Lizzie as happy a woman as she was herself. When the time was ripe.

In the meanwhile, there was nothing wrong with an excursion in mixed company with her half-brother and cousins. It was Christmastide, after all, and their guests were an unexpected gift.

CHAPTER 4

The tenth day of Christmas

On the pavement overlooking the river, the awed and festive crowd gathered to watch the tumblers, leaping fearlessly from one another's shoulders and rolling merrily about in britches and shirtsleeves, careless of the January cold. At braziers, sellers of hot chestnuts and mulled wine cried their wares, the delicious scents hanging in the air. At the four points of the compass, torches burned, enabling Maggie to see the sweat glinting on the young men's skin. She looked away, focusing rather on the defiance of gravity and speculating on the inevitability of broken bones.

"Rather a rough display for young ladies," Hugh commented beside her. "I had thought they would be better clothed, considering the temperature."

"Imagine the number of torn jackets and lost scarves in that case," Maggie pointed out. "When one is engaged in vigorous gymnastics, I do not suppose that propriety is the first consideration."

"You are right," he admitted. "I sounded like a prig, didn't I?"

Maggie smiled absently, her attention drawn yet again to Sydney, tall and even more handsome, if that were possible, in a greatcoat that made his shoulders seem broader, his carriage more dignified. He pointed out to Lizzie a particularly daring leap and even named it.

Tigg nudged her from behind. "Are you enjoying yourself, Mags?"

"I think it's wonderful," she said, her gaze still on Sydney. "I wonder if somehow these movements were not derived from those taught us by Mr. Yau. The ones on the ground, at least, seem familiar, don't you agree?"

"I do." Tigg nodded, and playacted a similar movement.

"I say," Hugh exclaimed. "Do you know those lads—the tumblers?"

"Not at all. But Maggie and Lizzie and I know something of their training, I think."

"How is that possible?" Now they had Sydney's attention, as well, which was quite the miracle, since he had been monopolizing Lizzie from the moment they'd boarded the Underground carriage.

"The first engineer aboard *Lady Lucy* taught us all something of his art of defense," Tigg told him. "It has come in useful more than once, and employs movements of the legs and arms similar to these."

"I should like to see a demonstration," Sydney said, as though Tigg had challenged him outright.

"Should you?" And before any of them could move, Lizzie had taken his arm, blocked his foot, and laid Sydney flat upon his back on the pavement.

"Great Caesar's ghost," he said breathlessly, gazing up at her. "How did you do that?"

"Lizzie, for pity's sake, you could have hurt him!" Maggie knelt next to Sydney and offered him her hand.

But Sydney waved her away and clambered to his feet unassisted. "That's a jolly good trick, and from a girl, no less." He dusted off his coat and retrieved his derby, which had rolled a little distance away.

"I wouldn't go underestimating the girls of our acquaintance," Evan murmured, gazing at Lizzie while no doubt remembering a similar occasion from the previous summer. "You'll only come to grief."

"I wouldn't dream of it," Sydney said, which made Maggie frown, because he just had.

Never mind. How could a man think clearly when he had just been laid out? What a lucky thing the Lady wasn't here. She'd have had Lizzie bundled back onto the train with a flea in her ear about her conduct in public, and so close to their debuts, too. Imagine if word got back to Lady Dunsmuir, who was to be their sponsor!

But her cousin, satisfied at having made her point, took Tigg's arm with one hand and Claude's with the other and between them, strolled away. This seemed to be the signal for their party to leave, so Maggie tossed a coin in the spittoon placed upon the pavement for that purpose, and hurried after them.

To her enormous pleasure, both Hugh and Sydney offered their arms to her at the same moment, and with only a second's hesitation to choose between them—for Hugh had been very kind in making conversation with a stranger—she took Sydney's arm.

This left Hugh, Evan, and Jake to bring up the rear of the little procession, which was probably the better option. Knowing Jake, he and Sydney would have come to blows by the time they reached St. Paul's. So really, she had accomplished two good things at once.

"Are you enjoying what you've seen of London, sir?" she asked, since Sydney did not seem inclined to speak.

"We've seen it before. This is our third visit, but our first on our own."

"Oh, I see. What part of it do you enjoy most?"

"Meeting lovely ladies." He smiled down at her, but she got the impression he'd said such a flirtatious thing because he believed she expected it, not because he really thought so.

"It seems a shame to waste a thousand years of history, in that case." She meant to tease him gently, but it took a second for him to get the joke.

"History is not wasted on me, I assure you. Though I am a man who prefers the present to the past. I look forward rather than back, as we tend to do in the Fifteen Colonies."

"I should like to visit there one day," Maggie said. She could smell his cologne now, as his temperature rose with the walk. She hoped he didn't notice her occasional deep breath as she tried to identify and then memorize it. "Do you live in Philadelphia, and see your cousin regularly?"

"We do, and I expect we shall when we return. I, for one, will make myself more of a presence at the Meriwether-Astor Munitions Works in future. It is, after all, my duty."

"Are you employed there? Our guardian, Lady Claire, was employed at the Zeppelin Airship Works for a time, but I cannot say that it agreed with her."

"Employed? Dear me, no. Our father had a position on the

board before he died, and as his eldest son, the seat passes to me." He glanced over his shoulder at his brother. "Hugh and I are in agreement that the enterprise needs a firm hand now that both he and Uncle Gerald are gone."

"I am sure that your cousin is providing it," Maggie said. "She wrote not long ago of an upcoming board meeting. I am sure that you will see her there, if you return in time."

"A board meeting, you say?" Maggie felt the muscles tense beneath her hand. "When is this?"

"I do not remember, precisely. It was to be about a week after Twelfth Night and the reception. Did you not know of it?"

"That would be just like her, to call a board meeting when we are on the other side of the world. Hugh, this is an outrage."

Hugh laughed. "Be fair, old man. Even if she sent a message, it would have a difficult time catching up with us. Remember, we have been on the move for several weeks, never staying in one place more than a night or two."

"If she wanted us there, she would have found a way. Why, even now she might be planning to oust us, and take control for herself."

"I understood that she had sole control," Lizzie said cheerfully. Maggie and Lizzie both rather enjoyed this fact, as they, along with Claude, were the heirs to their grandfather's shipping company, and thus had something in common with Gloria. "She was her father's only heir. Or are we mistaken?"

"You are not mistaken in the particulars," Sydney said reluctantly. "But in principle you are deeply in error. Our uncle ought not to have left the company in the hands of an inexperienced female. I cannot imagine what was in his mind.

Perhaps his time underwater in those infernal undersea dirigibles affected his powers of cognition."

"I doubt it," Maggie said soothingly. "I have traveled in one of his ships myself, and there was nothing lacking, from oxygen necessary to breathe to excellent food upon the table in the galley."

"You have?" He pulled away a little. "How on earth did that come to pass? I did not know that you were acquainted with my uncle."

Maggie could not very well tell him that she had been impersonating the man's daughter at the time, in order to rescue Claude, who had been kidnapped, so she said merely, "Oh yes, we attended several social affairs in one another's company in Venice. Be assured that the undersea dirigibles were very safe. I understand that Gloria has recalled them all from the Mediterranean and put them to work along your eastern seaboard."

Now he did drop her arm in astonishment. "Impossible!"

"Why should it be? The pigeon would simply find the vessel's signal when it surfaced, and deliver the orders without delay."

"Not that—impossible that she would recall them when the situation in the Adriatic is so … complicated."

"As to that, I have no knowledge." *That any of us are free to share with such new acquaintances, at any rate.*

"What about the Royal Kingdom of Spain and the Californias, then, since you seem to know so much of Meriwether-Astor affairs?"

Hurt, Maggie slowed her steps, and Jake drifted up beside her as though he had been waiting to do so for the entire quarter mile. "Mind your tone, mate," he said quietly. "I'll not allow anyone to speak to Miss Polgarth that way."

Evan flanked her on the other side, silently offering his support.

"I do apologize," Sydney said, as automatically as one might if one bumped into someone at church. "I only meant that—well, that clearly I need to renew my correspondence to Philadelphia. I feel rather wrong-footed in my lack of current information."

"You might inquire of Lady Claire," Claude said. "She and Gloria are thick as thieves, and letters fly back and forth as though there were merely a duckpond between them, not an entire ocean."

"Duckpond or ocean, to a pigeon it likely makes no difference," Hugh said, clearly trying to lighten the mood as well. "Shall we stop in at this public house for some refreshment? I swear that smelling those chestnuts and wassail has got me craving food—and we learned in our travels never to pass up a good opportunity."

Sydney's good humor returned, to Maggie's relief. But she no longer felt quite so inclined to attach herself to his side and hang on every word. Hugh and Evan seemed willing and more than happy to entertain her, though Jake never once relinquished his watch over both brothers. Lizzie, for her part, seemed entirely taken up with Tigg in the corner of their grouping of leather-covered chairs. If this didn't open Sydney's eyes to the fruitlessness of his attentions to her, nothing would.

Maggie determined not to allow her own partiality to be quite so visible henceforward. She certainly didn't want to be publicly rebuffed again, and Hugh's gentle admiration and

Evan's nearly inarticulate support were quite pleasant as a balm to ruffled spirits.

They were quite a merry party when they returned to Carrick House, and joining a lively game of charades with the younger ones left Maggie breathless with laughter. It was only when she slipped upstairs to fetch a comb for a prop (their word was *catacomb*) that she realized Sydney was missing— and that lamplight showed under the door of the Lady's study when the Lady was downstairs.

Quietly, Maggie turned the handle and opened the door on its silent and well-oiled hinges.

Sydney Meriwether-Astor stood over the Lady's desk, going through the papers upon it with an air of such distraction and worry that it was no wonder he did not see her. As Maggie watched silently, he found a letter that interested him. Scanning the lines quickly, he frowned, and dropped it, biting his lower lip.

Maggie stepped into the room and the click of the latch was his first indication that he was no longer alone.

He froze, staring at her, his hand arrested upon the pile of letters.

Maggie's blood, which had halted in horror, began to beat in her veins as defensiveness on the Lady's behalf struggled with the possibility, however remote, that he might have an explanation for being there. But her voice was calm. "Are you looking for a prop for the charades, too?"

His mouth tilted up in an embarrassed smile, and he stepped back with his hands clasped behind him. "I say, Maggie. You gave me quite a turn."

"I saw the light under the door, and those of us who live

here knows that Lady Claire does not permit anyone in her office uninvited but Mr. Malvern."

"Dear me." The color began to return to his face. "I am so sorry—I had no idea. I do beg Lady Claire's and your pardon most humbly. You are quite right—I was looking for a prop. With my lack of success here, perhaps we might remove to another room where I might find something to do with the word *stamp*?"

"I am sure we can. Mrs. Morven keeps a pocketbook full of stamps in her office downstairs, to which all of us have access." She stood to one side and indicated that he should pass her.

"Maggie?" came the Lady's voice up the stairs. "Did you find what you were looking for?"

"Yes, Lady," she called. "I'll be down in a moment."

Sydney paused on the landing. "You know, Maggie, perhaps there is no need to disturb Mrs. ... Morven, is it? I believe it would be more efficient simply to treat the word as a verb rather than a noun. To be honest, I should have thought of that before."

"Oh, that is a good idea. The children will enjoy it much more, especially if you lay it on thick."

"Then I shall oblige the children." He made no move to go downstairs and do so, however. "You won't mention my error to Lady Claire, will you? I feel dreadfully embarrassed—as though somehow I have let down the family, all over a silly stamp for a game."

He looked so miserable that Maggie's suspicions softened. "We all make mistakes, and how were you to know of the house rule? I shall say nothing."

For really, no harm had been done. His picking up of

letters and envelopes could be explained as easily by the search for a stamp as by a motive more inquisitive. For what would he gain by such brief glimpses of the Lady's correspondence?

At last his face relaxed and the handsome good humor returned. "You're a peach—one with a gift for making a man feel better about himself. I cannot say that of many girls."

He reached out, and with one finger, smoothed a tendril of hair away from her cheek.

But to Maggie's surprise, her heart did not skip a beat. Nor did she feel the urge to gasp, or to sway into his arms, as the tender look in his eyes invited her to do.

No, she merely felt embarrassed for him, for taking this second liberty quite uninvited. She stepped back and swung open the office door a little. "I'll just see to the lamp," she told him. "Tell the others I'll be down directly."

When she heard his footsteps on the stairs, she blew out the lamp. But not before she unfolded the letter he had examined and scanned it briefly.

Dearest Claire,

Thank you so much for your thoughts on the management of men of affairs, attorneys, and others who, in their attempts to help one, often muddy the waters of what exactly is the right thing to do.

I feel I have now come to a conclusion, and all that remains is to present it to the board of directors. They are to meet for the first time since Father's passing on Tuesday, January 14, where a motion will be made to officially create me president of the company. Apparently without such a motion, the banks will not act upon the terms of Father's will.

I in turn will move to make some changes among the members of the board to streamline things and—yes, only to you could I confess this—oust one or two of the members who are more inclined toward conflict than is healthy for the company.

For I believe Father has been delivering arms and igniting wars all over the world simply to make money. I cannot live with this. The Royal Kingdom of Spain and the Californias is the last unresolved problem, and if I have to go out there and spike my father's guns myself, I will do so, heaven help me.

Give Maggie and Lizzie and Alice my love. You four, I feel, are my sisters in efforts and adventures that seem to have amounted to a mission for world peace. I only hope that my part will be as successful as yours has been.

With my great affection,
Gloria

When Maggie came downstairs a few moments later with the comb, she found that, instead of continuing the game, Sydney and his brother were in the midst of making their farewells. Despite her surprise, she gave them her best wishes and assured them both of a waltz on Twelfth Night, and they took their leave.

It would be churlish of her to tell the Lady of such a small thing, and possibly damage the cordial relationship that they enjoyed now with the Meriwether-Astor family.

When she confided the whole story to Lizzie later that night, her cousin was as puzzled as she, and yet nodded at her decision. "I don't see that it would do the least bit of good to tell the Lady," she told Maggie, leaning on one arm in her bed. "He made an honest mistake, and it did no harm."

"But he did read her correspondence—at least, I saw him reading one of her letters."

"Did he? Or was he merely trying to determine how to get a stamp off the paper for a prop? Our adventures have made us suspicious, Mags, but Sydney and Hugh are gentlemen. We cannot go about accusing the poor boy of snooping and publicly embarrassing him, when he told you himself what he was doing."

Maggie nodded reluctantly and blew out the lamp. It didn't feel right, but then, what did she know of young gentlemen?

The only thing she knew for sure was that her brief infatuation with Sydney Meriwether-Astor had gone as inexplicably as it had come.

CHAPTER 5

Twelfth Night

*A*lice Chalmers stood just outside the door of the sitting-room, where the entire Hanover Square party were gathered before the landaus were brought round to take them to the ball at Hatley House. She took a deep breath, squared her shoulders, and stepped into the room.

Both Ian and his brother-in-law, Lord Blount, rose to their feet, and Ian, resplendent in his aeronaut's regimentals, medals upon his chest, took her gloved hand and kissed it.

"I have never seen you look more beautiful, my love," he said as the hot blood fanned into her cheeks. "Mother's sapphires suit you as though you were born to them."

They were rather a lot to live up to. But they lay upon her collarbones quite comfortably—far more comfortably than the tiara, which still rested in its case. "Claire sent Maggie over earlier to help with my hair," she said.

"She is to be complimented, then." He smiled into her eyes. "You look like a queen."

Indeed, the unruly mass did rather resemble a crown, braided into a coronet and stuck with so many pins that if she strolled close to a magnet, she would be wrenched against it with a clang. Together, she and Maggie had decided that the family tiara would be unsuitable for a woman not yet married, and had settled for tucking the brooch from the parure into the back of the roll instead.

The leaf-green silk of the gown with its waterfall of lace over the bodice was not so pale as to look young, and not so dark as to look matronly. It was the only evening dress she possessed—a gift from her father the last time she'd seen him—but thankfully no one need know that. And no one would be looking at the dress anyway—not with these sapphires.

She greeted the family, kissing the air next to the ladies' ears so that no one's earrings were caught in anyone's lace or hair. Even Lord Blount, whom she'd only seen in passing in the days since they'd arrived, complimented her on being "a fine-looking girl, a credit to the family."

It was all she could do to stifle a laugh.

Frances accepted her kiss with a smile. "You look lovely, Alice—though it is a shame your modiste could not match the color of Grandmama's jewels."

Alice came within a breath of asking, "Is the dress supposed to match?" but she caught herself in time. "I suppose it's only to be expected that modern fabrics would not match stones of such a great age," she said instead. "And I do not concern myself with such trifles in any case, do you?"

While Frances might not have come up with a reply, Lillian was already armed and ready. She kissed Alice, and then whispered, "Your coiffure is already coming down at the back. Do go make some repairs at once. I shall hold off Mama. You know how she is."

But when she reached her room, a worried glance in the mirror told her that Maggie's handiwork was made of sterner stuff. By the time she added another hairpin, just to be on the safe side, the landaus had pulled up and she realized she was going to make the whole party late. For Lillian had not held off anything except a triumphant smile at her expense as they puttered away, leaving Alice and Ian to bring up the rear.

Trifles. Not worth spending a single moment on. You have bigger creeks to cross.

Hatley House was lit from stem to stern, its huge expanse set in a garden the size of a city block, glittering with snow and lanterns strung all along the drive. Alice had known that the Dunsmuirs knew how to throw a party, but she'd never seen anything like this.

"One can certainly tell the occasions to which His Highness is expected," Ian murmured as he helped her out of the landau and offered her his arm. "This is magnificent."

Alice devoutly hoped that His Highness would never see fit to grace Hollys Park with the royal presence. She'd never survive the preparations and would collapse in a quivering heap in the receiving line before he could say hello.

The music of the orchestra met them before they were fairly in the door. Ian handed her cloak to a footman and they paced to the head of the staircase, behind his sister's party.

"Lord and Lady Blount, and the Misses Frances and Lillian Blount!" announced the majordomo in stentorian tones.

"Deep breath," Ian murmured, and stepped up to give the man their names.

"Captain Sir Ian Hollys and Captain Alice Chalmers!" rang

out over the assembled company, and they descended the stairs, backs straight, and smiling.

"That wasn't technically correct," she said to him out of the side of her mouth. "The Admiralty will not be pleased."

"The Admiralty can stuff it," he said through a charming smile, and it was all she could do not to giggle right there in front of everyone—and fall another fathom deep in love with him.

"Alice, how lovely you look." Lady Dunsmuir, rather than shaking her hand, took her into her arms for a hug. "And Ian, one may certainly say there is something about a man in uniform if *you* are the subject of discussion."

"No one holds a candle to you, Davina." Ian bowed over her gloved hand, on which rested a tawny diamond the size of a chestnut, no doubt the product of the Firstwater Mine.

Alice did not miss the expression on Lady Blount's face as she took in the familiarity of the countess's greeting of Alice in comparison to the politeness of her own. But Alice did not bother looking at the girls to see their reactions, for they simply no longer mattered. She was with her family again, in all this crush and glitter and music, and her spirits soared.

"Are Claire and Andrew here yet?" she asked the earl eagerly.

"We expect them at any moment," he assured her. "Stars above, Alice, don't you clean up well."

"As do you, sir." She dimpled at him.

"Thank goodness for regimentals," the earl said sotto voce, shaking Ian's hand. "At least one is sure to be wearing the right thing for these occasions."

"Thank goodness one has a wife to see to the situation,"

the countess said over her shoulder, accepting a curtsey from a lady Alice did not know.

And then something prompted her to turn just as Claire and Andrew appeared at the top of the stairs. Claire clutched Andrew's arm just as tightly as ever Alice had clutched Ian's, and on a warm tide of sisterly recognition, Alice remembered that Claire did not favor large gatherings like this. No matter that she and her husband were the guests of honor, or that they were both recognized by royalty in two countries, Claire would still much rather be in a laboratory, puzzling out a mechanical problem, just like Alice.

"Lady Claire and Mr. Andrew Malvern," boomed the majordomo. "Miss Elizabeth Seacombe and Mr. Claude Seacombe. Mr. Evan Douglas, R.S.E., and Miss Margaret Polgarth. Messrs. Stephen and Jacob McTavish. Mr. Lewis Protheroe and Mrs. Abigail Protheroe. Mrs. Rowenna Morven."

"Heavens, did she bring the boot-black along, too?" drawled a languid voice. Alice turned and recognized that insufferable Mrs. David Haliburton, with whom Claire had once gone to school.

With a gasp, the woman beside Mrs. Haliburton clutched her arm. "Hold your tongue, Catherine. What is she *wearing?*"

The color drained from Mrs. Haliburton's face and she gasped in her turn. "Julia. Tell me my eyes deceive me. Tell me that is not—"

"It is. Claire Trevelyan is wearing *a Worth gown*—and from this season's collection, too!"

Mrs. Haliburton made a sound a little like a whimper. "I cannot believe it. Oh, look at the satin. How beautiful it is! It's called *candlelight*, you know, because every woman looks well in it."

"There are few women who could afford to look *that* well," Julia said on a sigh. "The tucking. The lace. The pearls! Oh heavens, I fear I shall faint with sheer envy."

"I say, is that your friend Claire?" said the gentleman on Julia's other side. "She's become quite the looker, what?"

"Robert!" Julia snapped, and smacked him on the arm with her fan.

But Alice knew that the woman now embracing Davina did not owe her looks to Mr. Worth or even to any accident of genetics. Claire, after all, thought herself to be moderately attractive, but certainly no beauty. No, the glow in her eyes and the dimples in her cheeks were due to sheer happiness—in her accomplishments, in the company of her friends, and not least in her choice of husband.

Upon the arrival of the guests of honor, the earl had evidently decided he'd had enough of standing in the receiving line. After greeting her and Andrew and their party, he offered his arm to Claire. "Will the bride honor me by opening the dancing?" he asked, and swept her into the ballroom. Davina paired off with Andrew, and Alice found herself in Ian's arms, whirling to the strains of a waltz from *Der Rosenkavalier* before she could fairly take a breath.

"Aren't we supposed to wait for the Prince Consort?" she asked. Talking and dancing at the same time was still a struggle, but Ian was so practiced and smooth that with him, it was much easier than it would have been, say, with the earl.

"His Highness is not obliged to arrive on anybody's schedule but his own," Ian said. "We, however, are obliged to wait until he does, for it would be the height of rudeness to leave before he has made his appearance."

"How would he know if anyone left?"

"I am not speaking in general terms, but in the particular. I seem to recall he has requested a dance with a certain young lady other than the bride."

"Oh dear." Alice had completely forgotten that he had asked for a dance with her. "I swear, Ian, there are days when I wish I was back in Resolution."

"Are there, dear?" He gazed into her eyes, his hand at her back moving them effortlessly through the dancers. "Truly?"

"Once in a while, when this life starts behaving like the flash floods."

"This has been a rather trying week, I will admit. I shall be glad to see the trees of Hollys Park coming into view under *Swan*'s hull tomorrow."

"We are going home tomorrow?" What a relief! To be back on her own ship again, to see the familiar landmarks floating below, even to see those rascally French hens that she was getting acquainted with to see if they would become as friendly with her as Holly and Ivy were with Claire … she saw the value now of such simple gifts.

"Does that please you?"

"Oh, yes."

"So you are easier in your mind about the quiet country life?"

Again her gaze met his. "Life in the country is far from quiet. What about the wedding calls? The harvest festivals? The dinners and church fetes?"

His brows rose a fraction with each trial she enumerated. "What are you talking about?"

Claire had been right. "See? These are the kinds of things that Lady Hollys is responsible for, which Sir Ian has no idea of. Sadly, I have no idea how to manage them either. One of many reasons I've been, as you say, uneasy in my mind."

"Hang all those things." Somehow he had managed to dance her over to the French doors, which opened on to the terrace. The air was cold, but for the moment it was welcome on her hot face. "Who told you that the lady of house had to manage all that?"

"Claire."

"If Claire ever organized a church fete in her life, I'll eat my flight goggles. Why is she inflicting such things on you?"

"Mrs. Andrew Malvern might not, Ian, but Lady Flora St. Ives certainly did, and so did your mother. Claire grew up knowing what those expectations were. I didn't."

As he stared at her, her pleasure in the thought of going home began to dim at the edges as the reality of her situation flooded in again, like the tide at the shore. "You didn't know she did all that, did you?"

"Of course I did. Mother was always managing things and planning this, that, and the other in the neighborhood. But it did not seem to give her pause."

"Because she was brought up to it. Where does one even start organizing a harvest festival? Do you know?"

"Haven't the least idea. There are tents, and jugglers, and tables of food, I remember."

"Where does one obtain a tent?"

"One does not need to know. One orders one's land agent to manage it."

"Is that what your mother did?"

She could see he was becoming impatient with this

fictional harvest festival. How would he feel in October, when she was drowning in details and frantic because she had no idea where one got a bloody tent?

"I think you are making a mountain out of a mole hill," he said at last. "To the devil with all those things. The world will get along perfectly well without them, and meanwhile, we will be making our lives to suit us and no one else."

She allowed him to sweep her back onto the dance floor, and after the polka, Snouts asked her to dance, and then the earl, and then a gray, discreet sort of gentleman whose name was Arundel—Claire's solicitor and man of business.

But even as she smiled and made what conversation she could, Alice was thinking. It was all very well for Ian to say those things didn't matter, but even in Resolution, if someone had told the town's inhabitants that the New Year's fireworks and annual drunk were to be cancelled, there would have been a riot. Imagine what would happen in an English village, where traditions like these had been going on for generations. Maybe even centuries. You didn't just cancel a tradition because you didn't feel it was important.

The real question was, could she live up to the legacy of Lady Hollys? How badly did she want to be Ian's wife when that shadowy individual might not actually have that much in common with her, Alice Chalmers?

Or could a woman own her future in much the way she did her present? Was she even doing that? Or was she simply marking time until she figured out the right thing to do?

Why had she said yes to Ian in the first place?

I said yes to the man, not the baronet.

Then maybe she had done him a disservice. For with Ian, one could not separate the man from the baronet, or even the baronet from the aeronaut. He was all three, as easily as Davina was mother and countess and … whatever else Davina was. Society hostess. Royal confidante. Behind-the-scenes manager of politics and prime ministers.

Was such a life possible for Alice—to be air pirate's daughter and baronet's wife and airship captain, all in one? Or was she doomed to only manage two out of three, and in losing one lose a part of herself?

CHAPTER 6

*A*t a signal from the majordomo, the orchestra fell silent and a single trumpeter stepped forward in the dress uniform of a lieutenant. He blew a fanfare and in the final notes, His Royal Highness Prince Albert stepped to the head of the stairs.

Along with everyone else in the Hatley House ballroom, Claire and Andrew sank into curtseys and bows. And then like a lightning bolt of realization, murmurs spread across the room in a wave as the prince turned, held out his hand, and Queen Victoria herself, resplendent in diamonds and royal purple silk, stepped into view at the head of the stairs.

The orchestra swung into "God Save the Queen" as Claire tried to hold the curtsey. This was unheard-of, that Her Majesty should attend a bridal reception—and of people as insignificant as she and Andrew! Dear heavens, she was going to faint. Or be sick.

No, no. That would never do. For with a gesture, Her Majesty invited the company to rise, and Claire sucked in deep lungfuls of air as she did so. The spots cleared and she wished she had not asked Lizzie to lace her quite so tightly.

"All right, darling?" Andrew murmured. "We must go and be acknowledged. I am not sure I will survive the honor. Is my tie on straight?"

Fortunately, the royal couple were greeting the Dunsmuirs, which gave Claire about five seconds to see both herself and Andrew to rights, to straighten her spine, and to progress in as dignified a manner as possible toward the foot of the stairs.

"Lizzie, Maggie, Tigg—with us, if you please," she murmured as they passed. "Jake and Snouts—Lewis—you too."

"Holy Christmas in a cracker, Lady, you can't mean it!" Snouts croaked, while Jake's face lost all color.

"Now," she told them in her best Lady St. Ives tone, and meekly, they fell in behind.

"Your Majesty," Davina said, smiling, "I have the greatest pleasure to introduce to you the pair whose marriage we celebrate tonight. May I present Lady Claire and Mr. Andrew Malvern? Lady Claire is the sister of young Viscount St. Ives, her father the late Vivyan St. Ives, and her mother is Lady Flora Jermyn, of Cornwall. Mr. Malvern is quite possibly the best known of the Royal Society of Engineers, and I venture to say even His Royal Highness has read his monographs."

Claire sank again into her deepest curtsey and Andrew into a bow that nearly bent him in half. "We are deeply honored, Your Majesty," Claire managed from a dry throat. "I do hope this happy occasion finds you in good health?"

"It does, my dear," the Queen said, her voice throaty and low.

She was a tiny woman, her beautifully dressed hair gray, but her figure was trim from riding and dancing, and her gaze sharp with intelligence. "Do our eyes deceive us, or is that a Worth gown?"

"It is, Ma'am. A gift from a friend."

"We should all have friends with such taste. Mr. Malvern, we understand that you have recently invented a membrane for the airship that draws its power from the sun."

"Yes, Your Majesty."

"We trust that the patent for this remarkable invention will stay here in England and not travel about—say, to our dear relations over in the Kingdom of Prussia?"

"Yes, Your Majesty."

"Excellent. We do like a man of decision. Lady Claire, you may present these young people to us, and then we wish to dance—first with our husband, and then with yours."

"I believe that is my cue to ask you for the second waltz, Lady Claire," the prince said with a smile, "in memory of a similar dance at the Crystal Palace five years ago."

"I should be honored, Your Royal Highness." Claire curtseyed again, and then turned to indicate Lizzie and Maggie. "Ma'am, Sir, may I present my wards, Elizabeth Seacombe and Margaret Polgarth." They sank into curtseys so smooth that Claire silently blessed their Elocution and Deportment teachers at the *lycée* in Munich. "My former ward, Lieutenant Thomas Terwilliger, now serving aboard *Lady Lucy*."

Tigg bowed with the special flourish used by members of the Corps to the prince, their Commander in Chief. The prince's forehead wrinkled. "Correct me if I am wrong, Lieutenant, but I believe we have met before—at the same occasion at the Crystal Palace of which I just spoke."

"Yes, Sir," Tigg said. "I was helping to demonstrate the

Kinetick Carbonator built by Mr. Malvern, who was then my employer."

"Quite right. And how is your career in engineering progressing?"

"I have the honor to be second engineer aboard *Lacy Lucy*, Sir. Thank you for your recommendation. I was able to study and take the Corps engineering examinations because of it."

The prince beamed. "Excellent. And who might these gentlemen be?" The royal gazes moved along the line.

"My secretaries, Stephen McTavish and Lewis Protheroe," Claire said.

On the fringes of the room, an elderly voice could be heard to quaver, "Is that my Lewis? Being presented to the Queen? Blimey, Mrs. Morven, I shall faint!"

"And navigator Jacob Fletcher McTavish, currently serving aboard *Swan*."

"Simply *Swan*?" Her Majesty enquired while Jake looked as though his knees were not going to hold him up until he'd completed his bow. "Not *HMAS Swan*?"

"She is unregistered as yet," Claire said smoothly, with a glance over her shoulder for Alice.

"I believe there are two members missing from your party, Lady Claire," the prince remarked at this, looking over the assembled company. "I am to have the pleasure of dancing with one, I believe."

"That would be *Swan*'s captain, Sir," Andrew said. "Here they are now."

Davina said, "Your Majesty, Your Royal Highness, you are already acquainted with Captain Sir Ian Hollys, most recently commander of *Lady Lucy*, are you not?"

Ian bowed deeply, with the flourish, and reached behind

him to draw Alice forward. "It is a pleasure and an honor to see you again, Ma'am. Sir."

Alice was white with nerves as well, and her imploring gaze found Claire's. A tiny frown knit itself between Claire's brows. This was more than nerves. Something was going on of a deeper nature.

"May I present my fiancée, Captain Alice Benton Chalmers, formerly of the Texican Territories," Ian said proudly.

Alice sank into a curtsey, and only wobbled a little when she came up out of it.

Queen Victoria's gaze narrowed. "Captain, you say? Of *Swan*, an unregistered vessel?"

"Yes, Ma'am," Alice whispered.

"But how can you be a captain? Women are not permitted to fly in the Royal Aeronautic Corps."

Now Alice really did look as though she would faint. "I'm sorry, Ma'am," she whispered.

"For what? For using a rank to which you are not entitled?"

The crowd fell silent in horror at so public a rebuke. In the back, near the door to the refreshments room, someone young and female giggled.

It was this triumphant sound, and not the Queen's question, which caused Alice to visibly straighten and her chin to come up. "*Swan* is a Zeppelin B2 military-grade vessel, Your Majesty, which, as you say, I am not permitted to captain in the Royal Aeronautic Corps because of my sex. As a Texican, I find this puzzling, given that the Corps serves a country with a woman as its head of state."

Gasps rose about the room, and the Queen's eyebrows rose likewise.

"It strikes me as illogical that a woman may rule a nation, but she may not captain her own ship. For I have no doubt that there are as many men milling about in government as ever pulled up ropes and greased the engines of Your Majesty's fleet."

An appalled silence fell as the crowd waited to see what the Queen would do. Even the orchestra leader's baton hung loosely by his side as he became a spectator rather than a performer.

"You do express your opinions decidedly, do you not, Miss Chalmers?"

"I did not wish Your Majesty to labor under the mistaken impression that I claimed a rank to which I was not entitled." Alice's voice trembled even as she plowed on. "For I am entitled to it, Ma'am. I have earned it with pain and loss and years of experience."

"We see." The royal gaze shifted to Ian. "And you support your future wife in this?"

"I do," he said bravely. "My greatest fear is that she will choose the title of captain over that of Lady Hollys, and I shall be forced to move to the Colonies."

The Queen's eyebrows rose nearly into her hair, and even her diamond tiara shifted. And then—

—she laughed.

The tension snapped and a titter rippled through the crowd.

"We have been accused of many things," Her Majesty said, "but illogic is not one of them. Albert, dearest, we believe you ought to have a word with the Admiralty. We should not like it at all if Captain Hollys and his future bride were forced to relocate across the sea because of a rule that does not make sense, even to us."

"Of course, darling."

Davina sent a glance like an arrow toward the orchestra conductor, and the baton leaped into the air. The strains of the "Treasure Waltz," widely known to be Her Majesty's favorite, lilted through the air and the Prince Consort bowed to his wife. "Shall we?"

"With pleasure."

They sailed off into the center of the floor, which had cleared like magic, and Claire sagged against Andrew's side. She clutched Alice's hand wordlessly.

"I know," Alice croaked, as though Claire had spoken. "I can't think what came over me. She won't clap me in gaol for back-talking her, will she?"

Ian laughed, though it sounded a little unsteady to Claire's ears. "Hardly. It sounds rather the opposite—and if I were the Lord Admiral, I would be getting out paper and ink and drafting a bill for Parliament about the recruitment of female aeronauts, posthaste."

Davina leaned in. "He is in the card room. Do you wish Lord Dunsmuir to tell him, or must he wait to be summoned to the palace?"

"The latter," Ian said at once. His smile stretched a little wider. "I believe his department's treatment of Alice a few weeks ago merits such a summons in full."

The end of the waltz's first movement marked the moment when the royal couple could be joined on the dance floor without being thought presumptuous. Claire's foot was already tapping to the delightful music when Andrew whirled her out to join them, followed by Ian and Alice, John and Davina, and—to her chagrin—Tigg and Lizzie.

She lifted her brows at Lizzie in a silent remonstrance that communicated *What are you thinking? You are not yet out!*

Lizzie cocked her head toward the countess. *She said it was all right.*

And then Claire realized what had happened. In being publicly presented to the Queen, Lizzie and Maggie had effectively come out in society without benefit of balls, parties, or the prolonged sponsorship of Lady Dunsmuir over the months of the Season. In one fell swoop, the Queen had acknowledged them and cemented their acceptability and their place in society as Claire's wards and intimates of the Dunsmuirs.

When she saw Maggie dance past in Jake's arms, a sight that would have rendered Claire speechless in any other context now merely warranted a numb nod of acknowledgement.

Heavens. What a night. And it was only half over.

What else could possibly happen this evening to change the lives of those she loved?

"THANK you for asking me to dance," Maggie said to Jake as they waltzed past the Lady and Mr. Malvern. "I would have felt dreadful to have been left standing there when everyone else in our party was dancing."

"Thank you for saying yes," Jake said rather bluntly. "I've never asked a lass to dance in me life."

"You have so, when we practice in the parlor."

"Her Royal Bloody Majesty isn't in the parlor, and neither are all these nobs," he told her, moving her rather deftly around a portly gentleman and his wife. "I was never so frightened in my life, and that's saying something."

"You're not alone. And our Alice, speaking to her like that! I cannot imagine where she found the courage."

"I can. I've seen her in plenty of tight spots."

"But not like this. Not speaking up for herself in company —and royal company to boot. How proud the captain was of her! And how quick to back her up."

"I still can't see those two making a go of it," Jake said, which rather put a damper on her admiration. "She's as free as a gull and he's … well, he's not as stuffy as he used to be, but still, he prefers the life of a landed gentleman now. They're too different."

"I expect people said that of Her Majesty and the prince, too—or even of the Lady and Mr. Malvern. It is none of our business, anyway, Jake."

"It will be if she stops flying." He wasn't ready to give up the subject yet, Maggie could tell. "Then I'll be out of a job."

Ah, here was the real problem. "You could write the exams and join the Corps."

"Not me." A turn, then another. "I'm not the exam-writing kind. I do best in a situation like the one I'm in. The fewer to tell me what to do, the better."

Maggie had to admit that he knew himself pretty well, which was more than she could say for others—Mr. Sydney Meriwether-Astor, for instance. "That reminds me, I wonder if Sydney and Hugh came this evening?"

"I expect so. Any particular reason for you to be interested?" Jake gazed down at her curiously, and she blushed. No one but Lizzie knew of her accidental meeting with Sydney in the Lady's study, and Maggie preferred that it stay that way. For now.

"They do not know many people here but us, and after so many months of traveling, they may not be up to dancing."

"Too bad I didn't lay a wager, then." He turned her so that she was looking over his shoulder toward the door to the refreshment room. "For there they are."

How had she missed the announcement of their names? Perhaps, being Colonials, they did not realize they were to have given their names to the majordomo, and now they would have the trouble of introducing themselves. Well, it was none of her nevermind, as Alice would say. They could do as they liked. She was free.

Maggie sat the next one out—after all, who could resist watching the spectacle of Mr. Malvern dancing with the Queen, and the Lady with His Royal Highness? How lovely they looked, and how that nasty Lady Mount-Batting glow-ered and set wrinkles into her face! Maggie had written off Mrs. David Haliburton years ago as the sort who was never satisfied with anything, and had stopped paying her any mind. But tonight ... oh, tonight was deeply satisfying. To see the Lady achieve each of her dreams one by one—it was enough to make a girl resolve to aim high herself, so that the rewards that she could share with those she loved might be equally as satisfying.

Though Maggie could not really imagine a situation in which she would be rewarded by a dance with a prince.

Lizzie and Tigg came over then, and exchanged a smile that told her they were as delighted with the Lady's good fortune as she.

"I'm so glad it's her and not me," Lizzie sighed, watching them whirling around the floor.

Maggie had to laugh. Trust her cousin to find her delight in *not* having to share such good fortune!

The music ended, and after the royal couple danced with their host and hostess, and enjoyed a brisk polka with each other once more, the royal visit came to its end.

Maggie had never spent so much time in a curtsey in one evening before. What must it be like at court?

When the trumpet sounded a second fanfare from outside signifying that their carriage was trundling away, the atmosphere in the ballroom relaxed visibly into the gaiety of sheer relief, and the orchestra struck up a mazurka that had Maggie's toes tapping.

Evan asked her to dance, and then Claude, and before she could fairly take a breath, her card was full. When that occurred, of course, gentlemen began to cut in. Even Sydney only managed five minutes before he was interrupted. Gentlemen's faces blurred, her feet flew, and she became dizzy for want of something to drink.

And then Hugh Meriwether-Astor tapped her partner on the shoulder and she found herself in his arms.

"Why—Hugh," she said stupidly.

"Miss Polgarth, you are as white as a sail. Have you been danced to death like the Wilis in *Giselle*?"

"I don't think they were danced to death. The unfaithful gentlemen were. But yes, I am parched and half wondering if I shall faint."

"Come. Allow me to fetch you something."

It took three ladles of lemonade from the punchbowl before her mind cleared enough to allow her to speak sense.

"Thank you," she said simply. "I have never danced this much in my life. I should have realized one must pace oneself."

"You've been recognized by the Queen," he pointed out. "I understand from what some of the gentlemen have been saying that this is quite the social coup. As they say in China, you have gained enormous face."

"Dear me—that sounds as though I had been stung repeatedly by wasps," she said. "I merely had the luck to be in Lady Claire's party. She could hardly leave any of us out."

"You are too modest. I find such a quality in a girl delightful."

She averted her face and snapped out her fan to cool her overheated skin.

"It is certainly hot in the ballroom," he said, observing her closely. "Would you honor me with a turn about the terrace?"

"Oh, no," came out of her mouth before her mind could make itself up. "That would not do at all."

"There are several others outside. Just for a moment. You have gone from pale to flushed in an instant."

She could not fault him for his kindness. In fact, now that she thought about it, he had been consistently kind and she had been making such calf's eyes at Sydney that she had not appreciated it until now.

"Very well," she said at last. "Just for a few moments. Any more, and Lady Claire will send out the cavalry."

He offered his arm, and they strolled past the palms and out of the French doors on to the terrace. A quick glance at their company showed no sign of Lizzie or anyone else from Wilton Crescent, thank goodness. She did not need the razzing and speculation that Snouts and Lewis would be sure to dish out, nor the raised eyebrows of Lizzie and the Lady.

They stopped at a knee-high privet hedge and looked out over the small ornamental lake below, ringed by festive lanterns that cast pools of light upon the ice. What happened to the swans who made the lake their home when it snowed and froze over? Maggie hoped they had a warm nest in the reeds.

"There," Hugh said. "I'm grateful for a few refreshing moments I can look back on with pleasure. My time to harvest such moments grows very short."

"It does?" Maggie looked up at him. He was not as tall as Sydney, which meant she did not get a crick in her neck when she did so.

"Yes. My brother tells me we are to leave on the packet from Hampstead Heath tomorrow, and board the airship *Persephone* for New York on Wednesday."

Good heavens. This was as unexpected as their early exit from Carrick House the other evening.

"That seems a rather precipitate departure, does it not? And to take an airship rather than a steamer, as you have been doing during your whole voyage? Your brother said nothing of it the other night when we were all so merry together."

Hugh lifted one shoulder in a shrug. "He is most anxious to be home, hence the unprecedented choice of airship travel. Between you and me, I think he has a bee in his bonnet about our cousin and her plans for the company."

Sydney hadn't been looking for a stamp. He had read that letter as thoroughly as she had herself.

"Oh?"

"Somehow he has got it into his head that she means to cut him out of his board position—*our* board position—and stop the shipments to the Royal Kingdom of Spain and the Californias." He shook his head. "Where he could have got his information is beyond me. It can't be the newspapers, for I have seen nothing to make me come to any such conclusion."

"If this were indeed Gloria's intention, what would your thoughts be on the matter?" she asked carefully.

He chuckled. "I am a second son of a second son. I long ago decided that I would have to make my own way in the world, and depend on nothing but my wits and my own two hands. That is why I shall study the law when we return—specifically in the field of property conveyances and ownership of land. With the population so high in the Fifteen Colonies, land is a hot commodity. If people begin to look beyond the borders to the Texican Territory and even the Wild West, a man familiar with such things may make his living no matter where he is."

"I think you are wise. Wiser than counting on filling a dead man's shoes."

"You sound as though you had some experience in the matter."

"No, none at all. But I too have decided to make my own way. I have a little skill and the support of my family in the field of genetics, and plan to make it my life's work."

"You don't say." He gazed at her in admiration.

Maggie was not used to such attentions, so she kept her gaze fixed upon the ornamental lake. "My grandfather began a breeding program among Buff Orpington poultry that has become famous in Cornwall, and I shall continue it, publishing papers as soon as I am settled. There is so little known about the subject that I quite relish the chance to begin. I shall study the sciences at university, of course, and specialize by the time I reach my fourth year."

"My goodness. You quite take my breath away. Are all English girls so brilliant and so confident of their own futures?"

"I do not know," she admitted. "But the ones in Wilton Crescent are."

"Then I wish you every success, Miss Polgarth."

A sudden impulse made her say, "Please. You must call me Maggie if we are to be friends."

"Are we to be friends?" he asked, his tone gentle. "I had rather thought your interest tended toward my brother."

"Then you were mistaken," she said steadily. "And a girl may have many friends. In our house, we say that good friends are so valuable that one cannot turn them away."

"It is a capital philosophy. I believe I shall adopt it for my own. I only wish my brother would do the same." He sighed. "He has had more practice in the turning away, I am afraid. I fear he will offend our cousin, and then where will he be? She may turn him out, and if she does, he threatens to overthrow her and take the helm at the munitions works himself."

Maggie felt a *frisson* of alarm that manifested itself in a shiver. "Goodness me. Does she know his feelings on the matter? Perhaps she could recall him to a more familial view."

"I doubt she does. He does not show it in public, of course, but he is so angry that if he does not cool off before we moor in New York, I shall have to take measures to slow him down. But come. You are shivering. We must return to the ballroom, and I will attempt to fend off your admirers long enough to dance at least half of this waltz with you."

Maggie agreed so quickly that he seemed gratified. But in reality she could hardly wait for the dance to be over, and claimed fatigue when someone else attempted to cut in. She retired from the floor and began to circle the room, pushing through the crowd.

An angry Sydney taking the fastest means possible to the Colonies, in order to confront Gloria before the board meeting? The consequences could be dire—and it sounded as though his own brother believed him capable of physical harm.

Maggie had to find the Lady. She would know the best course to set.

CHAPTER 7

*M*uch as she admired the Prince Consort for what he had done for the Wit cause in business and politics, Claire could not help her relief at the departure of the royal couple.

It was one thing to say or do something to scandalize the members of society; it was quite another to cause the Queen to raise her eyebrows.

Now she and Alice, Andrew and Ian had repaired to the refreshments room for a well-earned glass of something stronger than lemonade, just in time to see Maggie returning from the terrace with Hugh Meriwether-Astor.

Alice followed Claire's startled gaze. "Do you disapprove?" she murmured, helping herself to a raspberry ice and several cakes.

"It is not that I disapprove," Claire said slowly. "Maggie is quite capable of deciding who her friends should be. I am just a little uncertain about those two young men. She and Sydney were absent for quite a long time the other night, and Maggie has said not a word to me. That in itself is unusual."

"You should grill Lizzie, then, if you don't think Maggie will tell you." Alice bit into a cake iced with Claire's and Andrew's initials twined together in gold.

"I am hoping I shall not have to grill anyone. I expect I will be allowed into the confidence of one or the other before the week is out." She sighed, feeling the constriction of her corset against her ribs. "Is this not a lovely party?"

"Most of it has been," Alice said. "I feel a complete fool about some parts."

"Then you must not." Ian handed her a glass of what smelled like wassail made the old-fashioned way, and Claire took one from Andrew gratefully. "I believe you may have changed the lives of hundreds, if not thousands, of women all over the country."

"Do you think she really will have the prince change the law about women in the Corps?" Alice asked.

"Of course she will." Ian nodded emphatically. "In fact, I would not want to be in the Lord Admiral's boots when he is summoned into the royal presence. I suspect that 'because it has always been done this way' will not hold the water it once did."

"Change will not come overnight," Andrew warned her, "but with the prince being a Wit, I believe it will come sooner than it might have during the previous reign."

"Hopefully soon enough that I can make a living flying." Alice offered a tiny beef and mushroom pie to Ian, then took one herself.

"You do not actually have to make a living, dear," he said. "We may live quite comfortably at Hollys Park—it is a working estate, as you know."

"I know," she admitted. "But I'm not sure I'm ready yet to tie up for good."

Ian looked a little alarmed at this news, and Claire hastened into the breach. "But if you are accepted into the Corps, as a captain you may control your time in the air and on the ground. You may fly as often or as little as you like, especially if you are flying for the Dunsmuirs."

"What if I wanted to fly for myself? Or for Gloria?"

"I do not see why you should not," Andrew said. "Gloria has made it quite clear she would prefer that above all things."

"While you two are busy planning my future wife's voyages," Ian said with mock sternness, "may I remind you that—"

"Lady!" Maggie pushed through the crowd and hastened to Claire's side. "I am so sorry to interrupt, but I must speak with you immediately."

A chill plunged through Claire's stomach. If Hugh had said or done something to upset Maggie, she would not answer for his immediate future. "Of course, darling. Let us move into the anteroom, where it is less crowded."

As though they sensed something more in the air than mere girlish gossip, Andrew, Ian, and Alice followed them into the small room lined with books, which Claire knew Davina used occasionally to meet callers who preferred not to be announced. Its occupants strolled away, leaving them in sole possession, and by habit they gathered around the hearth, where a cheerful fire flickered around the last remains of a Yule log. Tomorrow it would all be swept away, the decorations taken down, and the new year officially begun.

"What is it, Maggie?" Claire asked gently. "Did Mr. Meriwether-Astor offend you in some way?"

Maggie blinked at her. "Hugh? Oh, no. Nor did Sydney … at least, not directly."

Claire waited, her silence speaking volumes.

Maggie bit her lip. "I did not want to say anything, because what would be the point if they were not staying here long? But now I fear that may have been a mistake."

"Go on," Andrew said. "We have not had a repeat of your interview with young Justin Knight, have we? For if we have, I'll trounce the bounder myself."

Maggie shook her head, making the curls at her nape dance. "I found Sydney in Lady Claire's study the other night when I went upstairs to look for a comb for charades."

"My study?" Claire exclaimed. "Why, the impertinence! I hope you told him the house rule."

"I did. He said he was looking for a stamp for the charades also, but now I believe he was looking for letters from Gloria."

Claire felt quite breathless with offended indignation. "How rude and underhanded! I shall make it known at once that those two are not to be received."

"Hugh has done no harm, Lady. He has been lovely to me, and in fact, it is his information just now that sent me looking for you." Maggie's amber eyes were earnest. "They are leaving tomorrow on the packet, and taking *Persephone* from Paris on Wednesday. Sydney is in a tearing hurry to return to Philadelphia before Gloria holds the board meeting."

"Why should Gloria's affairs be anything to him?" Claire demanded. "He is not running the company."

"There is something strange going on. Hugh says that his brother is convinced Gloria is going to oust him from the board, and stop the shipments of arms to the Californias."

"That is precisely what she has confided to me—and I see

in your face that you know it, too. Never mind, Maggie—I would have gone back to see what he had discovered, too. Hugh clearly does not know that his brother has been reading my letters."

"No, and I did not enlighten him."

"I shall be happy to do so—when I have his lordship's footmen toss them both out of this house," Andrew put in grimly. "How dare Sydney show his face here and go about among our friends as though he were a gentleman?"

"But the point," Maggie went on doggedly, "is that Gloria must be told so that she is prepared for him. While I have no proof in the matter, I believe his brother thinks him capable of attempting physical harm."

"What?" Andrew's face darkened further still in a way that did not bode well.

"It is all right, Mr. Malvern." Maggie laid a reassuring hand upon his arm. "Do not concern yourself about any of us. Lizzie has already demonstrated the effects of Mr. Yau's training to him. It is Gloria, innocent and unprepared, whom I would wish forewarned."

"We must send a pigeon at once," Claire said. "From here, if we must. We have not a moment to lose."

"It won't do any good," Alice told her, setting her glass upon a nearby table. "The pigeons can't cross the entire Atlantic on their own. They go in stages, from ship to ship, until they get within range of land."

"I know that!"

"So what is the first ship on which they stage, in most cases?"

Alice looked at her expectantly, and with a cold chill of

knowledge settling into her stomach once again, Claire gave the answer. *"Persephone."*

"Exactly." Alice took a deep breath, and slipped her hand into Ian's. "That's why I'll take *Swan* and go."

"What?" Ian barked. His hand tightened upon her fingers as though he meant to stop Alice leaving there and then.

"If we really mean to help her, it's the only way. I'll pull up ropes in the morning, straight from the Carrick Airfield. *Swan* is so fast that I'll beat *Persephone* to New York by two days, and be in Philadelphia the day after. That will give Gloria time to prepare herself and the gentlemen of the board before Sydney gets there."

"This is outrageous!" Ian protested. "You cannot even think it, Alice. There must be another way."

"Name it," Alice said quietly, and when Ian sputtered and shook his head, she went on. "There is no danger. I'm simply being a pigeon myself, and carrying a message about a boy's temper. If I can be a moral support to her as well, then I'll be happy to stay a little longer to do what I can."

"But Alice—you are not prepared—" Claire began.

"*Swan*'s stores are full and all I have to do in the morning is visit the market for a few fresh things. Mr. Stringfellow is aboard, and Jake is here too. I have all the clothes a woman could want and then some. I need waste no time, and I'll be back next week."

"You seem to have thought this out rather thoroughly, for just having heard." From his tone, Ian was struggling to be reasonable. "But you must know that I cannot leave at a moment's notice."

"I'm not asking you to," Alice said softly. "I need some time. To think. To make sure I'm making the right decisions and not getting carried away by jewels and dances with princes, when real life might mean something quite different."

He gazed at her with such hurt in his eyes that Claire lowered her own gaze and turned her cheek into Andrew's lapel. They of all people could enter into this kind of pain, for they had experienced it themselves. But one could not simply say, "If you love each other enough, and put your beloved before yourself, it will all come right." This was the kind of storm that a couple could only weather when they didn't allow other people to take the helm.

"Don't look like that, dearest," Alice whispered, and went into his arms. "I'll be back before you know it, with this business settled … and my own mind settled, too. I promise."

"May I go with you?" Maggie asked, and Claire realized that she had quite forgotten her dear girl in her empathy for their friends.

"I don't think so, Maggie," Alice told her, and hugged her in her turn. "You and Lizzie have to go back to Munich soon yourselves, don't you?"

"This is more important than Munich."

"There I disagree. You and I have different courses to set, each equally important. And that's the way it should be. No, I'll have Jake and Benny with me, and together we'll see Gloria through."

Alice was standing taller, as though she braced her feet on *Swan*'s decks already—or was facing down a queen—and Claire knew that any arguments Ian might make would be blown away by the wind of her decision. If he was indeed fated to love strong women, as she had come to believe, then he would have to get used to living with one. As Andrew had.

And because she was a new bride and could command the

indulgence of society regarding displays of affection in public, she pressed herself to Andrew's chest and hugged him hard. It was the loveliest thing in the world when his arms came about her in return, as though he too was thinking along the same lines.

"What about you, Claire?" he murmured. "Will you go?"

If he had been the man he was this past autumn, such a question would never have crossed his lips. But he was not the same man, just as she was not the same woman.

"I would go if either she or Gloria needed me," Claire confided, "but they do not. I feel rather sorry for Sydney, truth be told. No, my place is here now, with you, and the children, and our plans for invention together."

And in the tightening of his hold she read his thankfulness, his appreciation of what those words meant to her, and above all, his love.

Love had given her the choice, and in freedom she had chosen. She could wish nothing greater for her friends.

CHAPTER 8

The next morning, after breakfast and a quick trip to the market, as many of the Carrick House inhabitants as could be wedged into the landaus puttered out to the airfield, where they became Alice's ground crew while she performed her flight checks. No one from Hanover Square came to see her off, but that was fine by Alice. Claire and Andrew would take Ian back to Hollys Park in *Athena*, and do their best to calm his mind about her sudden decision to fly away across the ocean.

She was at the stern, listening to the music of the great Daimler steam engines at idle and signaling Mr. Stringfellow to test the vanes, when she spotted a lone figure loping across the field, carrying a valise. When he saw her, he waved.

Evan Douglas? What on earth? Did he think Lizzie and Maggie were going with her, and meant to see them off?

"Captain Chalmers," he said breathlessly, rocking to a stop in front of her. "I just heard you were going to the Fifteen Colonies. Is that true?"

"It is." He was dressed in a canvas driving coat, and driving goggles sat upon his shabby hat. Surely he didn't intend to—

"I beg of you, please allow me aboard as a passenger. I am quite willing to pay, and to work as well, during the crossing."

Her jaw sagged in astonishment, and it took an effort of will to get her mouth operating properly. "Mr. Douglas, I don't know you very well, but even you have to admit this is … sudden." In her experience, young men tended to flee the country for only one reason. "Are you in trouble?"

"Not technically."

"It's legally that concerns me."

"Oh, no. Not at all."

She eyed him, but he met her gaze steadily. "I believe in honesty, and in beginning as I mean to go on. You can't tell me you're 'not technically' in trouble and expect me to cart you across the ocean without an explanation."

He'd regained his breath now after his dash across the field. "It is a matter of conscience. For in my small way, I helped in the affair of the telescope at Colliford Castle. You are familiar with the circumstances?"

She nodded.

"I cannot seem to get past it. The guilt of what I helped to create is crushing me—has been since the summer. If I do not do something extreme—something extraordinary—I fear I shall do harm to myself or another."

This did not sound good—and she was the last person in whom he ought to be confiding. "Mr. Douglas, no one believes you had anything to do with Charles de Maupassant's attempt to assassinate the Prince of Wales."

"They do not know. Please. I cannot bear the thought that between that and the experiments on poor Lizzie, I might have used science—the thing I revere most—to cause actual harm. Please let me assist in some small way, even if it is only washing dishes or—or bearing the notice of your arrival to Miss Meriwether-Astor once we moor. Please. I beg of you."

Alice gazed at him. There was no time to argue, and in any case, she could hardly blame a man for wanting to make things right, whether they'd gone wrong in reality or not.

"Very well." She pointed down the length of *Swan*'s fuselage. "The gangway is there. Man the levers and be ready to pull it up after I board."

For a moment she thought he might seize her hand and kiss it in some awkward fashion, but he did not. Instead, for the first time since she'd met him, a smile warmed his expression.

"Thank you. I am grateful. I'll do anything you ask."

"You might regret saying that when your turn comes to scrub the galley. Have Mr. Stringfellow show you where to put your case."

Shaking her head, she finished her checks and met Ian at the foot of the gangway for their last embrace. "I have a paying passenger," she told him.

"So I see. I cannot say that I am sorry you have another man aboard. I believe he can be trusted. Claire certainly seems to think so, and he is, after all, the Mopsies' cousin."

"If he can't be trusted, I'll toss him in the sea," she said lightly.

Ian tried to smile, but it was a poor attempt. "You will send a pigeon the moment you reach New York."

"I will," she promised.

"You will not allow yourself to be drawn into fisticuffs."

"Of course not. I have danced with a prince and am

engaged to a baronet. There will be no fisticuffs—but only because I have this." She half pulled her lightning pistol from the pocket of her canvas pants, and grinned.

"You will be the death of me," Ian said into her hair as he gathered her into his arms.

"I hope not," she said. She wished people wouldn't say things like that. They tempted fate.

"I have half convinced myself to abandon the estate and come with you."

"That would pretty much put paid to my ability to think," she reminded him. "Ian, don't be afraid for me. I was sailing the skies long before we met, remember? And Jake—"

"—is a dab hand in a fight. Yes, I know."

"Well, I am," came an indignant voice from above, where one of the viewing ports in the gondola was open.

"No eavesdroppers!" Alice called. "That's an order!"

"Fly safely," Ian said, his arms wrapped tightly about her. "Come home to me."

She had never felt so safe. But when he held her this way, she couldn't breathe. So she moved to put an inch of space between them, and kissed him deeply. "I will."

And then she turned and boarded, and while Evan pulled up the gangway as instructed, she climbed into the gondola where both Jake and Benny Stringfellow, her young midshipman, straightened and snapped a salute.

"Ready for lift?"

"Yes, Captain."

"Right then—to your stations, please. Mr. Douglas, come and join me to wave good-bye."

She leaned out of the viewing port into the cold January air. Below, Snouts, Maggie, and Lizzie stood ready at the ropes. Claire and Andrew, arms about each other, waved in farewell. Ian stood with one hand over his heart, keeping it safe for her.

Yuletide, with all its trials and joys, had slipped into the past, and the skies were clear and limitless, with just enough easterly wind to give her a helping hand down to Land's End.

"Up ship!" she called, and her friends cast off.

Freed, *Swan* spread her wings and fell up into fields of air. Alice smiled, welcoming the familiar pressure under her feet, and took the helm.

THE END

AFTERWORD

Dear reader,

I hope you enjoy reading the adventures of Lady Claire and the gang in the Magnificent Devices world as much as I enjoy writing them. It is your support and enthusiasm that is like the steam in an airship's boiler, keeping the entire enterprise afloat and ready for the next adventure.

You might leave a review on your favorite retailer's site to tell others about the books. And you can find print, digital, and audiobook editions of the series online. I hope to see you over at my website, www.shelleyadina.com, where you can sign up for my newsletter and be the first to know of new releases and special promotions. You'll also receive a free short story set in the Magnificent Devices world just for subscribing!

And now, in an excerpt from *Fields of Air*, we turn our thoughts to Gloria Meriwether-Astor, whose adventures are just beginning...

EXCERPT

FIELDS OF AIR BY SHELLEY ADINA

Philadelphia, the Fifteen Colonies
January 1895

She had not even been home a month, and she'd already had two proposals of marriage. This, it seemed, was the difference between being the heiress to a fortune, and the possessor of it.

Gloria Meriwether-Astor, guest of honor at a private ball hosted by the Main Line Hadleys, refused yet another offer of punch from a gentleman whose name she could not remember, and accepted the hand of Mr. Elias Pitman, one of the senior members of her father's board of directors.

"Thank you for the rescue," she said with a smile as he held her very properly and turned her about the ballroom floor in a sedate waltz. "One more offer of punch and I fear I shall turn it over the poor man's head."

"You are the guest of honor, my dear, and the wealthiest young woman in Philadelphia," he told her. "You could turn the entire bowl over his head and the newspapers would merely report that he had been impertinent to you. Tell me, are you tempted to accept either of the offers presently in hand?"

"Heavens, no. I have far too much to do to be side-tracked by matrimony."

"But you will be twenty-four in the summer."

Gloria remembered to keep her expression pleasant for the benefit of all who were watching. "You speak as though that were the end of the world," she said through a smile.

"Perhaps not, but the quarter-century may mark the end of such fine expectations as you enjoy now."

"Mr. Pitman, I have no doubt that my expectations, as you call them, have more to do with the size of my pocketbook than the depth of my wrinkles."

"You are a long way from that, my dear."

"Then let us have no more discussion of the subject." He turned her in front of the orchestra and whirled her back down the length of the room. "Instead, I wish to know what to expect on Tuesday, at the board meeting."

"Now?"

"Time is of the essence, and I wish to know your private thoughts, not those you may feel it is appropriate to express in front of others."

He was silent a moment. "Have you heard from your young cousins?"

"Not a word since Egypt."

"The notice of the board meeting was not delivered, to my knowledge. Despite quite astonishing advances in technology, one of the drawbacks of traveling so extensively is that communication becomes increasingly difficult. That will work in your favor, I believe."

Gloria nearly missed a step, and he covered for her admirably. "Why do you say that? Do you not like Sydney and Hugh?"

"I like and admire them both. However, Sydney would vote with Carmichael and Adams against you, and Hugh, regardless of his opinions, does not have a vote."

"Do you really believe Sydney would not vote for my confirmation as president?"

"Since he has no hope of that position, and it was your father's wish that you should take it up, I do not think there will be any difficulty on that score. No, my concern is for the ongoing matter of the Californias."

"That still leaves you, Mr. Stevens, and Mr. Bidwell. And my vote, once I am officially president, would break any tie."

"Carmichael is wavering. I have been working on him, but he cannot forget the glory days of last year, when shipments exceeded all our projections by such a margin that he lost his head and purchased a house on the Upper West Side in New York for his wife's use."

Gloria might have been no great shakes at mathematics in school, but her exposure to the business since had given her a keen understanding of profit and loss. And of the dangerous art of speculation.

"He is overextended."

"Yes, and with the failure of the French invasion of England, coupled with the disastrous closure of the English markets to the Meriwether-Astor ships as a result, he stands to lose it before his wife even has a chance to decide on wallpaper."

Mrs. Carmichael was a horrible snob who deserved to lose her house *and* its wallpaper just on general principles, but Gloria would never say so. Instead, she smiled at that lady as they passed, and received a strained grimace for her trouble.

"Can he be won over with a loan to stave off the immediate threat?"

Mr. Pitman's wrinkles creased into a smile over his high collar. "Spoken like a true Meriwether-Astor. How much would you propose?"

"Ten thousand ought to cover the wallpaper, at least."

"If it does not, then it would certainly stave off the jitters until your proposal to begin commercial shipping down the seaboard begins to bear fruit. That vote, at least, should be unanimous."

The waltz ended, leaving Gloria feeling more informed and slightly more nervous about Tuesday. For she had not confided even in Mr. Pitman about the proposal she planned once the lesser votes had taken place. They knew of her feelings about supplying arms to the Royal Kingdom of Spain and the Californias, of course. But what they did not know was that she planned to shut down the entire relationship and sever ties with that nation permanently.

No one but Claire knew that. And once Gloria was declared president, no matter what anyone said, she would do everything in her power to stop the conflict brewing on the frontier of the Wild West. A conflict ignited and prodded into existence by the pride of the Californios and the greed of her own father could not be permitted to flame into open war.

"And here is the Viceroy's ambassador," Mr. Pitman said, "ready to claim the next dance upon your card. He arrived only yesterday, bringing the last payment in order to take possession of the final shipment in person."

"In person?" Gloria's heart sank.

But there was no time to learn anything more. Mr. Pitman bowed and thanked her for the waltz, and then she found herself in the arms of Senor de Aragon y Villarreal. She had not known exactly who he was, when the young gentleman whom she now realized was his secretary had filled in his name on her card. She had only been amused that his name was so long it had run off into the margin.

She breathed deeply, attempting to convince her galloping heart to calm itself.

Senor de Aragon was a very handsome man in his early forties. He was dressed according to what must be the custom of his country, in a short black bolero jacket liberally encrusted with gold and silver embroidery, a shirt of dazzling whiteness, and trousers with silver medallions connected by fine chains extending down the outside of the leg. His black hair lay upon forehead and neck in romantic curls that had never seen macassar oil, and his eyes were so deep a brown that they looked nearly black in his tanned face.

"Miss Meriwether-Astor," he said, his voice a melodious bass. "I am honored to meet you at last in this so beautiful setting, which is still not enough to do justice to such a jewel."

Gloria blushed at the extravagance of his compliments. "You are too kind, sir. The Hadleys' home is very lovely."

"Your father did not tell us that he had a daughter so beyond compare. Please allow me to express my condolences. His death was a great loss to us all—the Viceroy wore black ribbons for an entire day."

"How very gracious and kind of him." Technically, she was

supposed to be swathed in black for another four months, but what would that signify? She could not honestly say that she mourned her father, despite his last heroic moments in giving his life for hers. Nor could she say that the world was a poorer place for his death. In fact, none of her confused sentiments regarding her father could be expressed to anyone—not even Claire.

So as was her habit, she expressed herself through her clothes. Her gown was lilac, the color of the final stage of mourning, with a nod to society's expectations in its black lace and ribbon trim upon the bodice.

She was not even supposed to be out in public. For that reason, because of the recent nature of her bereavement, the ball was a private affair. But Mrs. Hadley, who had been her mother's closest confidante, was far more concerned about marriage than mourning. And once one had Mrs. Hadley's approval, one had that of all of Philadelphia, and black crepe could go to the devil.

"You were personally acquainted with my father, sir?"

The Viceroy's ambassador swept her into the turns with a flair that suggested the swirling of a cloak rather than a woman. "I was indeed. He was a man of intelligence, of bravery, and of vision. He and the Viceroy spent many hours together, strategizing, conversing, and shooting. I suspect that in him, His Highness found the closest thing to a brother."

Lovely. Two warlike peas in an iron pod.

"Tell me of his vision," Gloria begged. "I am sorry to say that in recent years, I was not with him as much as I wished to be, and I regret the loss of such conversations as you describe."

He smiled down at her. Goodness, he really was very handsome.

"Ah, but as lovely as you are, it is not likely a man such as he would have taken a woman into his confidence."

Keep smiling.

"But I should still like to hear what he envisioned for the company. If I am to act as its head, I would hope that I might continue his legacy."

"A noble aspiration, to be sure." He gazed over her shoulder, but whether looking into the past or into the crowd, Gloria could not be certain. "You are familiar with the political situation in our glorious kingdom?"

"No, but I am anxious to learn, if you will tell me."

"Let us withdraw from the floor, then. These matters are somewhat complex, and require more attention than dancing will allow. Will you permit me?"

"Certainly. Let us walk in the conservatory."

Propriety dictated that she be chaperoned in the company of a gentleman, but Gloria's need to know as much as possible about the situation in the Wild West trumped such inconvenience. She hoped that Mrs. Hadley would not miss her for some time—at least until she had enough of the facts in hand that she could make good decisions on Tuesday.

In contrast to the snow and cold outside, and the crowded ballroom with its brilliant lights, potted palms, and chatter, the conservatory was warm and humid and silent, filled with all manner of flowers, vines, and pots of ferns and round shrubs. A row of orange trees set in the south windows were heavy with fruit that scented the air.

"Please. Be seated." Senor de Aragon indicated white wrought-iron chairs on either side of a breakfast-table, and

Gloria seated herself gracefully, her back straight, her expression interested as she arranged her skirts.

"I will share with you as best I can what your father learned in his visits to us, and you will see how important his role has been in the peace and prosperity of the people of the Royal Kingdom of Spain and the Californias."

Of certain people, at least. Rich people, who want to become richer.

"You have heard of the Texican Territory?"

She nodded, folding her hands in her silken lap. Alice Chalmers was from there—a town called Resolution. Gloria had looked it up and found it south of the capital of Santa Fe. Its claim to fame was its geography—set in the middle of a flash-flood plain, it had been left alone by settlers and government alike. Alice's stepfather, Ned Mose, found that this suited him just fine, air pirate that he was. He made his living wrecking airships, and the absence of both settlers and law, Alice had confided once, made the uncertain landscape both appealing and profitable.

"Perhaps you did not know that, two hundred years ago, most of the Texican Territory belonged to our glorious King?"

"No, I did not."

"Gradual incursion by movement west from the Fifteen Colonies has resulted in the Territorials setting up their own upstart government, intermarrying with once-loyal Spanish families, and the entire Territory seceding from Spain. All that is left now of a great kingdom is the thin strip of fertile land down the west coast, into the isthmus between the continents, and on to the northern shores and islands of the great southern subcontinent."

"Is that not enough for His Majesty?"

"When one has had the entire plate, it is difficult to satisfy one's hunger with only a slice of bread."

"And is His Majesty hungry?" Gloria asked the question with a twinkle of humor to soften its impertinence.

The Viceroy's representative twinkled back, clearly appreciating her femininity, if he did not appreciate her mind. "In a certain sense—if one realizes that the Texican Territory is said to be rich with gold."

Gloria's eyebrows rose. If that were so, why was Ned Mose not waylaying miners in the mountains? "Said to be?"

"One cannot discover the truth if one is not permitted to mine. Spain must have gold, and therefore it must have its lands back. This is where your father's vision and His Majesty's align most happily."

"I see," Gloria breathed. "The shipments of arms you have received thus far, then, have included guns, ammunition, train cars, articulated loading cranes for ore, and cannon."

His brows rose. "You are well informed."

"I looked it up." She gave him a sunny smile. "But there are entries for armaments which I do not understand. The final shipment, which I understand you will take possession of personally, contains many, many tons of iron comprising mechanics that seem to be raw materials, not completed machines."

How pleased he seemed with her knowledge!

"You are quite correct. The Meriwether-Astor Munitions Works has quite outdone itself in supplying the parts for the machinery that our scientists and engineers have created. Machines that, unlike airships, for instance, do not offend God, but rather emulate His own creation."

"In what way? Does not everything a man creates emulate that of God to some degree?"

"I see you are a budding philosopher as well as a great beauty." The warmth of his gaze might have been bestowed upon his own daughter. "I hazard to say that His Highness the Viceroy would enjoy talking with you as much as with your father."

"How very kind of you, but I cannot agree, I am sure. But the machines?"

"Have you ever seen the mechanical horses upon the—how do you call them? At the fair or the exhibition."

"The carousel?"

He snapped his fingers. "The carousel. Exactly."

"Why yes, I have. I spent many a happy day at the exhibition as a child, and the carousel was one of my favorite amusements."

"Picture those horses, not affixed to a pole, but as the cavalry of an army, invincible, and unaffected by weather or a need for food or water."

"The final shipment contains parts for mechanical horses?"

"*Sí, senorita*. And war towers borne on the backs of mechanical behemoths. And racing machines built to be faster than a cheetah, carrying rockets and bursting through offensive lines to release them into the heart of an army."

"Good heavens." Gloria felt quite winded, and her mind spun at the spectacle. "Would it not be simpler to sign treaties with the Texican government and split the yield from the mines equally?"

"There are no mines yet, and there will not be until the land is ours again," he said gruffly. "Land is our birthright—as any Californio will tell you."

"Californio?"

"The noblemen of our country—what the English call landed gentry. Many have titles extending back into the twelfth and thirteenth centuries, and families with roots in the titled nobility of Spain. We do not sign treaties. We own."

"I see," Gloria said thoughtfully, as though the prospect of mechanical animals and the annexation of perfectly happy territories minding their own business were normal. "And the Californio army is prepared, then, and ready to invade once the final shipment arrives?"

For the first time, his arrogant, proud gaze faltered, and he considered the orange trees with a frown, as though they were somehow lacking. "The Royal Kingdom does not have a standing army. But when the time comes, each landowner will raise men from his own acres to go and fight."

Gloria knew her history and geography as well as the next schoolgirl. It seemed rather feudal. "Is this the way they have always done it?"

"We have not needed to—not in two hundred years. Hence the growing necessity to make our wishes known to the upstarts and trespassers upon our ancestral lands."

"So ... no one has actually fought in two hundred years?"

"Not physically. But every Californio boy learns the strategies of war in the schoolroom, preparing him so that at any moment he may obey the King's will—in the person of the Viceroy—to rise up in his glorious name."

Gloria thought of the Kingdom of Prussia, where the army was an honorable career choice for any man. Or of England, where airships were registered with the Admiralty and, whether privately owned or not, crewed by trained aeronauts who could take to the skies to defend England's shores at a pigeon's notice.

So these Californios learned about war in school, but no one had actually fought in two hundred years? Were they mad? Or simply deluded by their own pride and grandeur?

"This is why our Viceroy's partnership with your father has been of vital importance," de Aragon went on, removing his censure from the orange trees and turning his dark gaze upon her instead. "We mean to declare war on the Texican Territory and take it back—and the Meriwether-Astor Munitions Works has made it all possible."

She was tempted to say, "About that—" but she could not. Not until she was officially president of the company, instead of merely its heiress. Instead, she offered as warm a smile as she could muster, and opened her mouth to say something inane and feminine and harmless.

The door to the conservatory opened, and she closed her mouth as Mrs. Hadley came in. "Gloria, dear? Are you in here?"

"Yes, ma'am." She stood, and de Aragon stood with her as Mrs. Hadley rustled over, splendid in burgundy silk. "Senor de Aragon y Villarreal and I were discussing some matters of business."

"Goodness, dear, that will never do. You sound just like your father—and half Philadelphia looking for a dance with you. If you will excuse us, Ambassador." Mrs. Hadley ushered Gloria toward the door with gloved hands that fluttered like birds. When they were out of the ambassador's hearing, she said, "I am bidden to tell you that you have a visitor. She is in here, in the morning room."

Gloria's heart leapt. Claire! "A visitor? Who could it be?"

On the threshold of the morning room she stopped short in stunned surprise, the skirts of her ballgown swirling around her feet.

"Will I do?" Alice Chalmers asked with a grin.

I HOPE you'll continue the adventure by purchasing *Fields of Air*. Fair winds!

Shelley

The Mysterious Devices series

The Bride Wore Constant White

The Dancer Wore Opera Rose

The Matchmaker Wore Mars Yellow

The Engineer Wore Venetian Red

The Judge Wore Lamp Black

The Professor Wore Prussian Blue

ROMANCE

Moonshell Bay

Call For Me

Dream of Me

Reach For Me

Caught You Looking

Caught You Hiding

The Rogues of St. Just by Charlotte Henry

The Rogue to Ruin

The Rogue Not Taken

One for the Rogue

PARANORMAL

Immortal Faith

ABOUT THE AUTHOR

Shelley Adina is the author of 24 novels published by Harlequin, Warner, and Hachette, and more than a dozen more published by Moonshell Books, Inc., her own independent press. She writes steampunk and contemporary romance as Shelley Adina; as Charlotte Henry, writes classic Regency romance; and as Adina Senft, writes Amish women's fiction. She holds an MFA in Writing Popular Fiction from Seton Hill University, and is currently at work on a PhD in Creative Writing with Lancaster University in the UK. She won RWA's RITA Award® in 2005, and was a finalist in 2006. When she's not writing, Shelley is usually quilting, sewing historical costumes, or hanging out in the garden with her flock of rescued chickens.

Shelley loves to talk with readers about books, chickens, and costuming!
www.shelleyadina.com
shelley@shelleyadina.com

Printed in Great Britain
by Amazon

86452091R00071